THE LOST ORPHAN OF THE PARISH

DOROTHY WELLINGS

CORNERSTONETALES.COM

1
HARDEST DAYS

Spring bloomed across St Michael's parish with shameless exuberance. Birdsong filled the air like scattered prayers, and the scent of wildflowers drifted through open windows. Ten-year-old Annabelle Sinclair sat leaning on the sill of her bedroom window, watching a robin hop around on the freshly turned soil. The world seemed determined to celebrate life while inside the house, everything whispered of its fragility.

Annabelle tucked a wayward copper curl behind her ear. Her hair—"just like your mother's," everyone said—refused to stay confined, much like her thoughts. She traced a finger along the rough stone, feeling its cool solidity beneath her touch.

The vicarage had always been a place of warmth. Sunlight still streamed through the windows, illuminating the same furniture, the same books, the same worn Bible on the side table. Yet something had shifted. The rooms that once bubbled with laughter now held only echoes.

Mother's embroidery hoop sat abandoned in her favourite chair, the needle frozen mid-stitch in a half-finished garden scene. Father's theological texts remained scattered across his desk, pages marked with notes in his careful script. The spaces between these abandoned projects felt heavier than the objects themselves.

Annabelle rose and moved to the parlour window. Her reflection stared back—earnest blue eyes that Father claimed held wisdom beyond her ten years. She never quite understood what he meant by that, only that when she asked difficult questions about God or heaven, he would smile and say, "Those eyes of yours see right through to the heart of things."

Through the glass, she spotted her mother sitting in the garden alcove. Susan Sinclair's thin shoulders were wrapped in her woollen shawl despite the mild day. Her hand rose to her mouth as a cough shook her frame—gentle at first, then more insistent. The sunlight caught her profile, highlighting how sharp her features had become, how pale her skin against the vibrant spring colours.

Father appeared at Mother's side, his tall figure bending solicitously as he offered a handkerchief. Annabelle watched his face—the worry lines deepening around his eyes, the forced smile that didn't quite reach them. His hand lingered on Mother's shoulder longer than usual, as if he could somehow transfer his strength to her through touch alone.

A knot formed in Annabelle's stomach, tight and uncomfortable. Something in Father's careful movements, in Mother's fragile posture, spoke of a truth no one had put into words.

Annabelle looked away from the window, drawing a deep breath. She slipped through the back door and crossed the garden path, her footsteps silent on the smooth stones. Mother's eyes brightened as she approached, and Father squeezed Mother's shoulder before excusing himself to prepare for Sunday's sermon.

"Come sit with me, my darling," Mother said, patting the stone bench beside her.

Annabelle settled next to her mother, careful not to jostle her. The bench felt cool through her cotton dress, but Mother's presence radiated a different kind of warmth.

"Your hair is wild today," Mother said, her voice thin but affectionate. She reached out with pale fingers to brush the unruly curls from Annabelle's forehead. "Just like mine was at your age. My mother used to say it was because I had too many thoughts trying to escape all at once."

Annabelle leaned into her mother's touch. "Do you think that's true?"

"Perhaps." Mother's fingers continued their gentle exploration, tucking strands behind Annabelle's ear. "Do you remember the stories I used to tell you about the girl with copper hair who could speak to birds?"

"She lived in a cottage at the edge of a great forest," Annabelle continued, the familiar tale flowing easily, "and every morning, the birds would bring her news from distant lands."

Mother smiled, her green eyes crinkling at the corners. "You always loved that one. You'd ask for it night after night."

"You never seemed to mind telling it."

"That's what mothers do—we tell the same stories over and over because they bring joy." Her hand stilled in Annabelle's hair. "And because we hope the lessons in them will stay with you long after the stories end."

Annabelle reached for her father's Bible that she'd brought outside with her. Its leather cover was smooth from years of handling, the pages well-thumbed and marked with ribbon. She traced the gold lettering on its spine.

"You taught me that faith isn't just about the grand miracles," Annabelle said quietly. "It's about finding God in small moments—like birds bringing messages or stories told over and over."

Mother's eyes glistened. "You listen so carefully. That's your gift, Annabelle." She took a laboured breath. "Remember that God speaks to us in whispers as often as in thunder. Sometimes His greatest strength shows in how we face our hardest days."

2
GARDEN THOUGHTS

Annabelle heard the sharp rap of the brass knocker echoing through the vicarage. Father's footsteps hurried across the wooden floor, followed by hushed voices in the entryway. Dr Harrison's distinctive baritone mingled with Father's more urgent tones as they moved toward Mother's bedroom.

Clutching her father's Bible to her chest, Annabelle crept toward the voices. The narrow hallway felt colder than usual as she pressed herself against the wall near Mother's room, her heart thumping wildly against the leather-bound book.

"I've done everything I can, Thomas." Dr Harrison's voice drifted through the partially open door. "The consumption has taken too firm a hold."

"There must be something—anything." Father's voice cracked. "Perhaps if we took her to London, to a specialist—"

"I'm afraid we're past that point. A week, perhaps two at most."

Something heavy thudded against wood—Father's fist

against the wall, Annabelle guessed. The sound made her flinch.

"Not even a month?" Father's voice had shrunk to a whisper. "Not even enough time to see the roses bloom."

Annabelle's fingers turned white around the Bible's edges. A week. Two at most. The words rattled in her mind like pebbles in a tin cup. Cold spread through her body despite the spring warmth filtering through the windows.

Dr Harrison murmured something about making Susan comfortable, about preparations that should be made. Father's responses came in short, clipped sentences, as if speaking full thoughts might shatter him completely.

When the bedroom door swung open, Annabelle darted back toward the kitchen. Father found her there moments later, staring blankly at the kettle.

"Annabelle, darling." His face looked carved from stone, eyes hollow. "Why don't you play in the garden while Dr Harrison and I speak with your mother?"

She nodded, unable to form words around the lump in her throat.

Outside, the sun continued to shine with cruel indifference. Annabelle wandered past the vegetable patch, past the apple tree where her swing hung motionless, until she reached Mother's rose garden. The bushes stood pruned and waiting, their first green shoots reaching toward the light, unaware that the hands that had tenderly shaped them might never see their blooms.

Annabelle sank onto the small stone bench, her father's Bible still clutched to her chest. Last summer, Mother had taught her how to deadhead the roses, showing her how to snip just above the five-leaf junction. "This is where new growth comes from," she'd explained, her fingers gentle on the stems. "Sometimes we must cut away what's finished to make room for what's to come."

3
ROSES

Dusk settled over St Michael's parish, casting long shadows across the vicarage garden. Annabelle remained on the stone bench, her small fingers tracing the gilded edges of her father's Bible. The evening breeze carried the scent of newly-turned earth and the promise of roses yet to bloom.

"Annabelle!" Father's voice cracked through the twilight. "Come quickly!"

She sprang to her feet, the Bible clutched against her chest like a shield. Her heart hammered wildly as she raced through the garden, past the apple tree, its branches reaching like desperate fingers toward the darkening sky.

The vicarage door stood ajar. Annabelle slipped inside, her footsteps thundering against the wooden floorboards. The hallway stretched before her, impossibly long.

"Annabelle," Mother's voice floated from the bedroom, fragile as moth wings. "My darling girl."

Annabelle burst into the bedroom, breathless. Mother lay propped against pillows, her skin nearly translucent in the lamplight, her copper hair spread across the white linen like autumn leaves on fresh snow.

"Come here, love." Mother patted the bedside with trembling fingers.

Annabelle crawled onto the bed, careful not to disturb the mountain of blankets despite the mild spring evening. Mother's hand found hers, cool and light as a fallen petal.

"My beautiful girl." Mother's words came between shallow breaths. "Let me look at you properly."

Father stood at the foot of the bed, his knuckles white where they gripped the bedpost. His face twisted with grief, eyes bloodshot and wild. He looked like a stranger, this broken man wearing her father's clothes.

"Thomas," Mother whispered, "come sit with us."

Father moved woodenly to the other side of the bed, taking Mother's free hand between both of his. His shoulders shook with silent sobs.

"I want you both to remember something." Mother's voice strengthened momentarily. "Love doesn't end. It changes shape, but never disappears."

Annabelle nodded, not trusting her voice. The room smelled of lavender water and illness, of endings disguised as ordinary moments.

"My copper-haired girl." Mother's fingers brushed Annabelle's curls. "Promise me you'll still speak to the birds."

"I promise," Annabelle whispered.

Mother's smile illuminated her face one last time, bright as sunlight through stained glass.

The room fell silent, a terrible stillness descending like dust settling after a storm. Mother's chest no longer rose and fell. Her hand, still entwined with Annabelle's, grew impossibly lighter, as if something essential had slipped away between one heartbeat and the next.

"Susan?" Father whispered, his voice cracking like thin ice. "Susan, please."

Annabelle stared at her mother's face. The lines of pain had smoothed away, leaving behind a strange, peaceful mask that looked both familiar and foreign. This wasn't Mother anymore—just the shell she'd left behind.

Father collapsed across the bed, his body convulsing with silent sobs. The sound that finally escaped him wasn't human—a wounded animal's cry, raw and primal. Annabelle sat frozen, unable to move or speak, her small hand still clutching her mother's cooling fingers.

Annabelle slid from the bed and moved to her father's side. Her hand found his shoulder, and she pressed herself against him, two survivors clinging to a piece of wreckage in a vast, indifferent sea.

"Father," she whispered, her voice steadier than she felt. "Father, I'm here."

Thomas turned to her, his face ravaged by grief, and pulled her fiercely into his arms. Annabelle breathed in his familiar scent of wool and paper and ink, anchoring herself to this one remaining certainty.

The vicarage creaked and settled around them, the familiar home suddenly strange and empty. Without Mother's laughter echoing through the hallways or her soft humming in the kitchen, the rooms felt cavernous, cold.

That night, Annabelle refused to sleep in her own bed. She curled beside Father in the chair by the fire, her small body pressed against his, as if her presence might somehow prevent him from slipping away too. When sleep finally claimed her, she dreamt not of death but of her mother's roses—how they'd been cut back to stubborn, thorny stems that would, despite everything, bloom again.

4
DIFFICULT DAYS

Annabelle woke with a start, her neck stiff from sleeping in the armchair. For one blessed moment, confusion clouded her mind—why wasn't she in her bed?—before memory crashed down upon her like a toppled bookshelf she remembered Mother was gone.

The fire had died during the night, leaving only cold ash in the grate. Father was no longer beside her. His absence sent a spike of panic through her chest until she heard the distant clink of a teacup, from the kitchen.

Morning light filtered through the curtains, casting long rectangles across the floor. It seemed wrong somehow that the sun should rise at all, that birds should sing and the world continue turning when Mother lay cold upstairs.

Annabelle pulled her shawl tighter around her shoulders. The vicarage felt different this morning—emptier, as if the walls themselves had expanded overnight, creating more hollow space to be filled with absence. Mother's presence had always made their modest home feel warm and full. Now the rooms echoed with what was missing: no humming from the kitchen, no soft footsteps in the hallway, no gentle voice calling Annabelle to breakfast.

She padded into the kitchen, her bare feet silent against the cold floor. Father stood at the window, staring out at Mother's garden. The morning light carved deep shadows beneath his eyes.

"Father?" Annabelle whispered.

He turned, his face softening at the sight of her. Without a word, he opened his arms. Annabelle rushed into his embrace, burying her face against his waistcoat. He smelled of tobacco and grief.

"I've made tea," he said, his voice rough from crying. "Your mother always said a cup of tea helps one face difficult days."

They sat at the kitchen table, the silence between them thick but not uncomfortable. Father reached across and took her small hand in his larger one.

"We'll find our way through this, Annabelle," he said, though his voice wavered. "Your mother's love remains with us, even now."

Annabelle nodded, remembering Mother's words. Love changes shape, but never disappears. She glanced toward the window where Mother's roses would soon bloom, pruned back last autumn to survive the winter frost.

5
WEEKS

Weeks slipped by in a haze of grief. Annabelle sat at the kitchen table, watching as morning light filtered through the draped windows of the vicarage. Dust motes danced in the golden beams, highlighting the stillness that had settled over their home since Mother's passing. The clock on the mantel ticked with solemn persistence, marking time in a world that felt suspended.

Father entered the kitchen, his clerical collar already fastened about his neck. Annabelle's heart tightened at the sight of him. Grief had carved new hollows beneath his cheekbones, and the skin around his eyes seemed permanently creased. His shoulders, once straight and proud, now curved inward as though bearing an invisible weight.

"Good morning, Annabelle," he said, his voice flat where it once held melody.

"Morning, Father." She pushed a cup of tea toward him. "I've made it just as Mother showed me."

Something flickered across his face at the mention of

Mother—pain, perhaps, or gratitude—before settling back into that mask of quiet endurance he'd worn these past weeks.

"Thank you, my dear."

Father sipped his tea in silence, then rose to finish dressing for Sunday service. Annabelle followed him to his bedroom, watching from the doorway as he stood before the mirror, adjusting his vestments with trembling fingers. The ritual was familiar—she'd observed it hundreds of times—but today, she noticed how deliberately he arranged his features, smoothing away the grief, straightening his posture, practicing a smile that never reached his eyes.

"The congregation expects their vicar to be strong," he murmured, more to himself than to her. "They need guidance, not my sorrow."

At church, Annabelle sat in the front pew, her eyes never leaving Father as he conducted the service. His voice rang clear through St Michael's, reciting prayers and scripture with practiced eloquence. To anyone who didn't know him well, he might have seemed merely solemn, appropriate for a man of God. But Annabelle saw what others missed—the absence of warmth in his tone, the mechanical precision of his movements, and the haunting emptiness in his blue eyes when they swept across the congregation.

The parishioners noticed too. Mrs Langs leaned toward her husband, whispering behind her prayer book. Old Mr Pitts shook his head sadly. Miss Aughton dabbed at her eyes with a handkerchief.

Father's sermon that day was on faith during times of trial. His words were perfect, his theology sound, but they echoed in the church like stones dropped into a well—resonant but hollow.

∼

ANNABELLE LINGERED at the doorway of her father's study, watching him from the shadows. Father sat hunched at his desk, quill suspended over parchment, droplets of ink bleeding into the paper beneath his unmoving hand. The shelves behind him—once meticulously arranged by Mother—now bore the marks of neglect. Books stood at odd angles, papers jutted from between leather-bound volumes, and a fine layer of dust coated everything except the chair where he sat day after day.

Sunlight streamed through the window, illuminating motes that danced through the still air. The vicarage had transformed since Mother's passing. Rooms that once bubbled with laughter and the gentle cadence of Mother's voice now held only silence, as if the house itself mourned her absence.

Annabelle stepped back, her stocking feet silent against the wooden floors. The corridors seemed longer now, darker. Mother's absence was a physical thing—a hollow space that followed Annabelle from room to room, pressing against her chest when she least expected it.

In the kitchen, unwashed teacups from breakfast still sat in the basin. Mother would never have allowed such disorder. She'd kept their home running with quiet efficiency, filling each corner with warmth and purpose. Now meals were forgotten, laundry piled in corners, and conversations had dwindled to sparse necessities.

Annabelle returned to the study doorway. Father hadn't moved. His Bible lay unopened beside him, its leather cover dulled from years of handling. Pages of sermon notes were scattered across the desk, crossed out and rewritten, then abandoned. The bottle of sat perilously close to the edge, threatening to topple with the slightest movement.

His shoulders rose and fell with each laboured breath. The black of his clerical clothes seemed to absorb the light around him, casting him in perpetual shadows. His fingers, once steady as he turned Bible pages or wrote his sermons, now trembled slightly as they hovered over the blank page.

The grandfather clock in the hall struck three, its sonorous chimes echoing through the empty house. Father flinched at the sound but didn't turn. The weight of his responsibilities—his congregation, his daughter, his faith—seemed to press him further into his chair, a physical burden bending his once-straight back.

6
VIBRANT MEMORIES

Annabelle sat cross-legged on the worn rug before the hearth, her father's Bible open upon her lap. Father occupied his armchair, shadows dancing across his gaunt face as firelight flickered against the growing darkness outside. This had become their nightly ritual—scripture readings where Father's voice strained to fill the emptiness Mother had left behind.

"Shall we continue with Psalms?" Father asked, his finger marking a page.

Annabelle nodded, though her eyes drifted to Mother's empty chair opposite Father's. The cushion still bore the slight impression where she'd sat evening after evening, her gentle voice bringing the ancient words to life.

"The Lord is my shepherd; I shall not want," Father began, his voice faltering slightly. "He maketh me to lie down in green pastures..."

The familiar words hung between them, hollow without Mother's soft interjections or thoughtful questions. Father read mechanically, as if reciting a shopping list rather than words of comfort. Annabelle's attention wandered to the mantelpiece where Mother's silver hairbrush still lay, untouched since that final morning.

"Do you remember," Annabelle said suddenly, interrupting Father mid-verse, "how Mother would read the story of Daniel? She'd roar like the lions."

Father's hands trembled slightly as he lowered the Bible. "She certainly had a flair for the dramatic."

"And when she read about David and Goliath, she'd grab the fire poker for David's sling." Annabelle mimed the action, swinging an imaginary weapon.

A smile cracked Father's solemn expression. "Your mother once knocked over a vase demonstrating that very scene."

"The blue one from Aunt Margaret!" Annabelle's eyes widened. "Mother told me it was the cat."

Father's laugh—rusty from disuse—burst forth unexpectedly. "She made me promise never to tell."

Annabelle giggled, the sound strange in the quiet house. For a brief moment, the room felt warmer, lighter, as if Mother's spirit had brushed against them.

Then silence fell, abrupt and heavy. Father's smile faded, and his eyes grew distant again. He cleared his throat, fingers fumbling to find his place in the Bible.

"Where were we?" he murmured, the brief connection between them already slipping away. "Ah, yes. 'He leadeth me beside the still waters...'"

Annabelle's shoulders slumped as she watched Father retreat back into himself, the memory of Mother's vibrant presence making her absence feel all the more profound.

7
WHISPERINGS

Annabelle lingered by the church door after Sunday service, watching Father receive the parishioners' sympathies. Mrs Oak pressed a covered dish into his hands while Mr Porter clapped his shoulder with uncomfortable vigour. Father nodded mechanically at their words, his clerical collar seeming to choke him as he forced polite responses.

"Such a shame," Mrs Wilkins whispered to Mrs Abbott, not quite beyond Annabelle's hearing. "The Reverend's wasting away before our eyes."

"The light's gone out of him," Mrs Abbott agreed. "Can't say I blame him—they were devoted to each other—but the poor child..."

Their gazes flicked toward Annabelle, who pretended sudden interest in straightening her gloves.

The whispers had begun three weeks after Mother's funeral. At first, they were sympathetic murmurs about Father's dedication—how admirable it was that he continued his duties despite his loss. Now, four months on, the tone had shifted. Concern laced with judgment. Pity tinged with impatience.

Father collected a stack of food parcels, his hands trembling slightly as he thanked the Widow Marsden for her generosity. The woman's eyes widened at his appearance—the hollowed cheeks, the sallow complexion that spoke of sleepless nights.

"Reverend, you must rest," she insisted. "God would understand if you took time to heal."

"The Lord's work continues, Mrs Marsden," Father replied, his voice a shadow of its former resonance. "My comfort comes from serving others."

But Annabelle knew better. Each sermon drained him. Each pastoral visit left him more depleted. He'd returned from visiting the ailing Mr Collins yesterday and collapsed into his chair, a coughing fit wracking his thin frame.

That morning, she'd found him at his desk, head resting on his arms, sermon half-written. When she touched his shoulder, he'd startled awake, disoriented, his skin burning with fever.

"I'm perfectly well," he'd insisted, though his hands shook as he straightened his papers.

Now, watching him struggle beneath the weight of the food parcels, Annabelle ached to help him—to somehow mend his broken spirit as he'd tried to mend hers. But Father had become a fortress of grief, the drawbridge raised against all comfort, even hers.

She stepped forward to take some of the parcels, noting how his coat hung loose where it had once fit snugly. Father offered a weak smile that never reached his eyes, and Annabelle felt a flutter of fear in her chest. The congregation might whisper about Father's broken heart, but Annabelle saw something more alarming—his body failing alongside his spirit.

8
PROMISES

Dr Harrison's carriage clattered up the vicarage drive, sending gravel scattering beneath iron-rimmed wheels. Annabelle watched from the parlour window, her breath fogging the glass. The physician's visits had become more frequent as Father's coughing worsened. Mrs Porter from the village had taken to bringing broth each day, her eyes filled with the same knowing sympathy they'd held when Mother was failing.

"He'll be wanting his tea strong today," Mrs Porter murmured, bustling about the kitchen. "Poor man barely touched yesterday's broth."

Annabelle slipped away before Mrs Porter could offer more pitying glances. She crept up the stairs, pausing outside Father's bedroom door where hushed voices filtered through the oak panels.

"—quite advanced, I'm afraid." Dr Harrison's tone carried the same grave cadence it had when discussing Mother's condition. "The infection has settled deep in both lungs."

"How long?" Father's voice sounded distant, as though already halfway to somewhere else.

A pause. "A week. Perhaps two."

Father's soft chuckle surprised Annabelle. "God's timing is perfect, even when we fail to understand it."

"Thomas, there are treatments we might try—"

"No, old friend. Susan waits for me."

Annabelle's knees weakened. She slid down against the wall, her chest tight with unshed tears. The door opened, and Dr Harrison started at finding her there.

"Miss Annabelle," he began awkwardly.

"He's dying," she whispered. Not a question.

The doctor knelt beside her, his weathered face solemn. "Your father has pneumonia, child. But between us—" he glanced toward the bedroom "—I believe his heart began failing the moment your mother left this world."

Annabelle nodded. She'd known it all along.

"He's asking for you."

Father lay propped against pillows, Bible open across his lap. Sunlight streamed through the window, catching dust motes that danced around his gaunt face. He looked peaceful—more at ease than he had in months.

"Come, little one." He patted the bedcover beside him.

Annabelle perched on the edge, taking his thin hand in hers. His skin felt papery, the blue veins prominent beneath.

"I've been writing something for you." He indicated several sheets of parchment on the bedside table. "Not quite finished, but—" a coughing fit interrupted him.

When he recovered, he squeezed her hand. "Your mother once said you had my eyes but her spirit. She was right." His smile reached his eyes for the first time since Mother died. "Promise me you'll keep that spirit bright, even when the world seems dark."

"I promise," Annabelle whispered.

9
TRULY ALONE

The vicarage became a place of whispers. Parishioners tiptoed through the hallway, bearing offerings of food that piled untouched in the kitchen. The scent of illness hung in the air—camphor and medicinal teas mingling with the musty smell of bedsheets too long unchanged. Annabelle divided her time between Father's bedside and the parlour where she received visitors with a composure that belied her ten years.

"Would you like me to read to you?" she asked one afternoon, perching on the chair beside his bed. Father's breathing had grown more laboured overnight, each inhalation a struggle against the fluid gathering in his lungs.

He shook his head weakly. "Tell me... about the garden instead."

Annabelle described Mother's roses, how the white ones had bloomed first this year, their petals unfurling in the spring sunshine. She spoke of the blackbird that had built a nest in the hawthorn hedge and the way the evening light turned the flagstone path golden.

"Mother always said the garden was where she felt closest to God," Annabelle murmured, stroking Father's thin hand. "Remember how she would stand with her face tilted up to catch the rain? She said it was like feeling His tears of joy."

A ghost of a smile crossed Father's pallid face. "Susan believed... heaven touched earth in that garden."

Each day, Annabelle sat beside him, recounting memories like precious beads on a rosary. She reminded him of the Christmas when Mother had surprised them with gingerbread shaped like theological texts, and how Father had laughed until tears streamed down his face. She spoke of summer picnics and winter evenings by the fire, Mother's voice rising and falling as she read aloud from favourite books.

On the sixth day after Dr Harrison's final diagnosis, Father's breathing changed. Annabelle recognised the rattle from Mother's last hours and sent for the doctor, though she knew his coming would change nothing.

Father's eyes flickered open as twilight painted the room in shadows. His gaze found Annabelle, blue eyes bright with fever yet suddenly clear. His lips moved, forming words too faint to hear. She leaned closer.

"So proud," he whispered. His fingers tightened briefly around hers before relaxing. "You have... her strength."

Annabelle held his gaze as something shifted in his expression—a mixture of recognition and release. His chest rose once more, then stilled. The hand in hers grew slack.

In the sudden silence, Annabelle felt the world tilt beneath her. Orphaned. Alone. The weight of it pressed against her chest, stealing her breath just as surely as illness had stolen Father's.

∼

ANNABELLE STOOD like a small statue beside the freshly-turned earth of her father's grave. The black mourning dress Mrs Marsden had hastily altered hung loose around her thin frame, the sleeves too long, the hem dragging in the churchyard mud. Rain fell in a fine mist, catching in her copper curls and beading like tiny crystals that refused to fall.

The village had turned out in force—faces Annabelle recognised from Sunday services now blurred into a sea of black coats and solemn expressions. Their whispers carried on the damp air.

"Both gone within half a year," Mrs Porter murmured to Mrs Oak. "Never saw a man waste away so quickly."

"The physician called it pneumonia, but we all know the truth," replied Mrs Preston, not bothering to lower her voice. "Died of a broken heart, he did. Couldn't live without his Susan."

Annabelle's fingers curled around the worn leather Bible in her hands—her father's Bible, with his neat annotations filling the margins. The only inheritance she had. Reverend Bloom, newly arrived to take over the parish, had conducted the service with efficient detachment, his words ringing hollow in the church where her father's voice had once filled every corner.

"Poor little mite," someone said nearby. "What's to become of her now?"

What indeed? Annabelle watched as the gravediggers began shovelling earth onto the simple wooden coffin. Each thud of soil striking wood reverberated through her bones, final and irrevocable. Father was gone. Mother was gone. The vicarage that had been her home for all her ten years would soon belong to another family.

The cold seemed to seep through her inadequate clothing,

settling deep in her marrow. She had thought herself prepared—had witnessed her mother's passing, had nursed her father through his decline—but standing here, watching the earth swallow him up, the finality crashed over her like a wave. Alone. Truly alone.

10
ARRANGEMENTS

Annabelle watched the new vicar stride through the vicarage as though he already owned every corner of it. Reverend Bloom moved with purpose, his polished boots clicking against the wooden floors her father had walked with gentle steps. He was tall with light brown hair neatly combed, his clerical collar pristine against his black coat.

"This will need to be cleared," he announced, gesturing to her father's collection of books. "Make space for more modern theological texts."

Annabelle clutched her father's Bible tighter. Something in Reverend Bloom's tone made her stomach twist—where her father had spoken with warmth and consideration, this man's voice held only cold authority.

"When might you be ready to vacate the premises, child?" Reverend Bloom asked, not looking at her as he examined her father's desk.

"I—I haven't been told where I'm to go, sir," Annabelle replied, her voice small.

His eyes narrowed as they fell upon her father's papers.

"What are these?" He picked up several pages of her father's neat handwriting.

"Father's theological notes. He was writing something before..." She couldn't finish.

Reverend Bloom's expression changed subtly. He thumbed through the pages, his eyes widening momentarily before he tucked them into his coat.

"I shall review these. The church must determine if any of these writings have value."

Later that afternoon, Annabelle pressed herself against the wall outside the parish council room, straining to hear the discussion within.

"The child cannot remain at the vicarage," Reverend Bloom was saying. "I require the space to properly establish my ministry. We must consider what's best for her future."

"Perhaps one of the families could take her in?" Mrs Marsden suggested.

"That would be a burden upon already struggling households," Bloom countered. "I've made inquiries. Thornfield Orphanage has space and would provide structure and discipline—precisely what a child in her position requires."

"An orphanage all the way in Thornfield seems severe," someone protested weakly.

"It is the most practical solution," Bloom insisted. "They will feed her, clothe her, and teach her a useful trade. What more could we ask? The parish cannot be expected to maintain her indefinitely."

Annabelle's heart hammered against her ribs.

"I've taken the liberty of making preliminary arrangements," Bloom continued. "For the child's welfare, of course. The sooner she can begin her new life, the better for all concerned."

11
FAREWELLS

Three days after the parish meeting, Annabelle stood in her father's study—no, Reverend Bloom's study now—watching as he sorted through her father's remaining papers with meticulous care. Outside, autumn rain pattered against the windows, matching the steady drip of dread that had pooled in her stomach since overhearing his plans.

"The arrangements have been finalised," Bloom announced, not looking up from the desk. "I met with the authorities at Thornfield yesterday. They've agreed to take you in next Tuesday."

Annabelle's fingers tightened around the worn leather of her father's Bible. "Must I go, sir?"

Bloom glanced up, his expression arranged into what might have passed for sympathy had it reached his eyes.

"My dear child, what alternative exists? A young girl requires structure, discipline, proper Christian guidance. Thornfield will provide all these things." He smiled thinly. "I've ensured you'll be well looked after. The orphanage master has promised to place you in the sewing room rather than the laundry. A much more suitable environment."

His words dripped with false concern that made Annabelle's skin crawl. As he turned back to her father's papers, she noticed how he separated certain pages, tucking them into his own leather folio.

Annabelle watched Reverend Bloom carefully fold another page of Father's notes into his leather folio. The rain had stopped, but water still dripped from the eaves, each drop a measured countdown to Tuesday's departure.

"You'll find Thornfield quite adequate," Bloom said, not looking up. "The master there runs a most efficient establishment."

Annabelle's throat tightened. "What of Father's writings? His sermons might comfort the congregation."

Bloom's fingers stilled momentarily. "These?" His voice lifted with practiced lightness. "Merely drafts, my dear. Unfinished thoughts. The congregation requires proper guidance, not fragments."

He closed the folio with a decisive snap and straightened a stack of papers on the desk—her father's desk, where he'd spent countless evenings crafting sermons that had moved parishioners to tears.

"I've been contemplating a series on divine providence," Bloom continued, eyes brightening. "The church requires fresh perspective. Your father's approach was... traditional." He smiled thinly. "I've discovered some fascinating theological concepts among these papers that, with proper development, could transform St Michael's standing in the diocese."

Annabelle's fingers curled around the worn leather of her Bible. "Father spent years developing those ideas."

"Indeed." Bloom's gaze flicked toward her, then away. "A pity he never published them. But the Lord works in mysterious ways, bringing light from darkness." He rose, tucking the folio under his arm. "The carriage arrives at nine on Tuesday. Pack only what you can carry."

That afternoon, Annabelle slipped into St Michael's, seeking solace in its familiar shadows. Mrs Marsden and Mrs Fitch stood near the altar, arranging flowers, their voices carrying in the empty church.

"Poor little dear," Mrs Marsden whispered. "Shipped off to Thornfield like unwanted baggage."

"What choice is there?" Mrs Fitch replied. "The new vicar needs the house, and no family has stepped forward."

"Still, sending her away seems so harsh. Thomas and Susan would be heartbroken."

Annabelle retreated to a back pew, a gnawing dread washing over her. The church had always been her sanctuary, but now even these stone walls felt foreign. She knelt, pressing her forehead against clasped hands.

"Please," she whispered, "show me what to do."

No answer came except the hollow echo of Mrs Fitch's voice: "The vicar says it's for the best."

When Sunday arrived, Reverend Bloom made the announcement from the pulpit, his voice ringing with authority.

"Our dear Annabelle Sinclair will be departing for Thornfield Orphanage, where she will receive proper care and training for a useful future. The parish has fulfilled its Christian duty in securing this opportunity for her education and welfare."

From her seat in the front pew, Annabelle fought back tears. The Bible in her lap—her father's Bible with his careful notes in the margins—was the only thing she would take of him. Everything else would remain behind, claimed by Bloom, who spoke of Christian duty while his eyes gleamed with something that looked nothing like charity.

The following morning, Annabelle knelt beside her small carpetbag, in the bedroom, that would soon belong to someone else. She folded her nightgown—too thin for winter—and placed it beside her second dress and spare stockings. Her fingers brushed against Mother's hairbrush, its bristles worn from years of taming copper curls identical to her own.

The carpetbag's contents were pitiful: two dresses, undergarments, a nightgown, Mother's brush, and Father's Bible. Ten years of life reduced to a bag smaller than the box that had held Mother's wedding china.

Outside her window, Mother's roses continued their stubborn autumn bloom, oblivious to the changing ownership of the soil that nourished them.

On Tuesday morning, Annabelle stood in the vicarage doorway, her small xarpetbag at her feet. Bloom waited by the gate where a plain black carriage had arrived, its driver impatient.

Annabelle turned, taking in the worn threshold where Father had carried Mother over on their wedding day, the sitting room where they'd read together each evening, the kitchen where Mother had taught her how to make bread. Each room held ghosts of laughter and whispered prayers.

"Come along, child," Bloom called. "Thornfield awaits."

Annabelle lifted her bag, the Bible secured inside, and stepped over the threshold for the final time.

12
THORNFIELD ORPHANAGE

The carriage slowed to a halt, its wheels grinding against gravel. Annabelle peered through the grimy window at the imposing structure before her. Thornfield Orphanage loomed against the grey sky, its stone walls rising like a fortress. The driver yanked open the door without ceremony.

"Out you get, girl."

Annabelle stepped down, her legs stiff from the journey. The air smelled of coal smoke and something else—despair, perhaps. A tall iron gate stood before her, its hinges rusted from years of minimal care. Two men in drab uniforms pushed it open with a screech that set her teeth on edge.

"Annabelle Sinclair?" One of them consulted a crumpled paper. "Follow me."

She followed, her small carpetbag bumping against her leg with each step. The courtyard stretched before her barren, save for puddles from the morning's rain. Children in identical grey garments shuffled across it in orderly lines, heads bowed. None spoke. None laughed. The silence pressed against her eardrums like cotton wool.

The contrast to St Michael's vibrant gardens and her father's warm study struck her like a physical blow. Here, colour seemed to have been deliberately scrubbed away, leaving only shades of grey and brown.

Inside, the corridors stretched long and narrow, punctuated by doors leading to rooms where the sounds of labor echoed—the rhythmic thump of looms, the scratch of brushes against stone, the clatter of pots. Children's voices, when they came, were muted and cautious.

"Mr Pullter will see you now," her guide announced, stopping before a heavy oak door.

The office beyond was sparse but warmer than the corridor. A man with a face like carved granite sat behind a desk piled with ledgers.

"Sinclair girl." He didn't look up. "I am Mr Pullter, master of Thornfield. Here you will learn discipline, industry, and gratitude. You will rise at five, work until supper, and retire at eight. Silence during meals and work. Speaking only when spoken to. Cleanliness is mandatory. Disobedience means punishment."

His eyes finally met hers, cold and assessing. "Your father's position affords you no privileges here. Is that understood?"

Annabelle nodded, words trapped behind the lump in her throat.

"Verbal response, girl."

"Yes, sir," she managed.

"Take her to the girls' dormitory," he instructed the waiting woman at the door.

Annabelle followed the matron up narrow stairs to a long room lined with iron beds. Girls her age and younger sat on them, folding linens with mechanical precision. Their faces turned briefly toward her—hollow-cheeked, with eyes that had forgotten how to hope. Some wore fading bruises. All wore the same expression: resignation.

One girl, thin as a winter reed, glanced up longer than the others. For a moment, something like curiosity flickered in her eyes before she returned to her task.

Annabelle's chest tightened. These children had stories like hers—lives interrupted, families lost. The weight of their collective sorrow pressed down on her shoulders, heavier than any trunk she could carry.

13
SURVIVING

The harsh clang of the bell tore through Annabelle's dreams each morning, jolting her from whatever brief solace sleep had offered. In the grey pre-dawn light, she and two dozen other girls scrambled from their beds, fumbling with buttons and laces while the matron barked orders. No time for prayers. No moment of quiet reflection as there had been at the vicarage. Just the frantic rush to avoid punishment for tardiness.

"Move faster, Sinclair!" The matron's voice cut through the dormitory. "Those floors won't scrub themselves."

Annabelle's knees pressed painfully against the stone floor as she worked the brush back and forth across the endless corridor. The lye soap burned her hands, turning them red and raw. She'd once had a child's soft palms; now callouses formed where the wooden brush handle rubbed against her skin. Each movement sent fresh pain through muscles unaccustomed to such labor.

She tried to recall her father's gentle voice reading scripture, but the memory slipped away beneath the scrubbing rhythm and the burning in her shoulders. The vicarage kitchen, once her domain for making Father's tea, now seemed like a dream from another life.

By midday, her stomach cramped with hunger. The dining hall, with its long wooden tables and backless benches, offered little comfort. Children filed in silently, eyes downcast as they accepted their bowls of thin gruel.

"Heads bowed in gratitude," Mr Pullter announced from the head table. "Remember, you eat by the charity of others."

Annabelle stared into her dented bowl. A few pale lumps floated in watery porridge. She remembered Mrs Marsden's kitchen at harvest time—warm bread with butter, apple tarts, roast chicken on Sundays. Her stomach growled audibly, prompting a sharp look from the matron.

"Something displeases you about your meal, girl?" the woman asked, her voice carrying across the silent hall.

"No, ma'am," Annabelle whispered, feeling dozens of eyes upon her.

"Then perhaps you'd like to express your gratitude to Mr Pullter for providing it?"

Annabelle swallowed hard. "Thank you for this meal, sir."

Satisfied, the matron moved on. Annabelle lifted a spoonful to her lips, forcing herself to eat despite the bland taste and gritty texture. Around her, children hunched over their bowls, protecting what little sustenance they received. No one spoke. No one smiled. They simply ate with mechanical efficiency, knowing this meagre offering must sustain them through hours more labour

Nights at Thornfield Orphanage brought little respite from the day's hardships. The dormitory air hung thick with the mingled scents of unwashed bodies and damp stone. Annabelle's narrow bed creaked beneath her as she shifted, careful not to disturb the other exhausted girls. Her fingers sought the familiar shape hidden beneath her threadbare blanket—her father's Bible, the sole treasure she'd managed to keep.

The worn leather binding felt warm against her palm, a stark contrast to the perpetual chill of the orphanage. Annabelle glanced furtively around the darkened room. The matron had completed her final inspection and retreated to her quarters. Only then did Annabelle dare to retrieve her precious book.

She pulled it from its hiding place and cradled it to her chest. The stub of candle she'd saved from her meagre ration cast a trembling circle of light as she carefully turned the pages. Her father's handwriting filled the margins—little notes, observations, and questions that made the ancient text come alive. Annabelle traced his neat script with her fingertip, feeling closer to him and her Lord.

"In my Father's house are many mansions," she read in a whisper so faint it barely stirred the air. "If it were not so, I would have told you."

The words blurred as tears gathered in her eyes. She could almost hear Father's gentle voice reading the passage during their evening devotions, Mother's hand resting lightly on her shoulder. The memory was so vivid that for a moment, the cold stone walls of Thornfield seemed to fade away.

Annabelle wiped her eyes with her sleeve and continued reading. The stories of Joseph sold into slavery by his brothers, of Daniel in the lion's den, of Esther's courage—they spoke to her now in ways they never had before. These were people who had endured, who had found strength when all seemed lost.

As sleep finally claimed her, the Bible rested against her heart. Her dreams carried her back to the vicarage garden, to Mother's roses and Father's laugh. But inevitably, the dreams twisted. The roses withered, the garden path stretched endlessly, her parents' faces receded into darkness.

Annabelle woke with a start, her heart hammering against her ribs. For a terrifying moment, she couldn't remember where she was. Then the reality of the orphanage closed around her like a fist. She clutched the Bible tighter, drawing comfort from its familiar weight and the knowledge that within its pages, she could find her way back to herself, to the love that had shaped her.

Days melted into weeks, weeks into months. Annabelle ceased counting time by dates and instead marked it by small mercies—a slightly warmer bowl of gruel, five minutes of sunshine during outdoor labour, or the rare night when exhaustion brought dreamless sleep.

One dreary afternoon, as she scrubbed endless rows of chamber pots, Annabelle found her mind drifting to the vicarage garden. The memory of Mother's roses bloomed vivid against the grey backdrop of the orphanage. She could almost smell their sweet fragrance, feel the velvet petals beneath her fingertips. Mother had taught her that roses needed pruning to grow stronger—the cutting back made them more resilient, more beautiful.

"Perhaps that's what's happening to me," Annabelle whispered to herself, scrubbing harder at a stubborn stain. "Being cut back so I might grow stronger."

The thought brought an unexpected comfort. Her parents hadn't raised her to wilt at the first harsh wind. They'd prepared her, though they couldn't have known for what. Father's voice seemed to whisper from the pages of his Bible each night: "Remember who you are, Annabelle. Remember whose you are."

She belonged to them still—to Mother's gentle wisdom

and Father's steadfast faith. Their love hadn't vanished; it had simply changed form, just as Mother had promised.

On the worst days, when Mr Pullter's temper flared and the matron's cane fell swiftly for the smallest infractions, Annabelle retreated to the sanctuary of her mind. There, Father's words echoed: "In faith, there is hope."

She'd repeat it silently while scrubbing floors until her knuckles bled, while chewing tasteless gruel, while lying awake listening to the muffled sobs of younger children. In faith, there is hope. The mantra steadied her when her arms trembled with fatigue and when hunger gnawed at her belly.

The words became her armour against despair, a reminder that this place—these stone walls and iron rules—could contain her body but not her spirit. Each morning as the bell clanged her awake, she silently renewed her promise: to survive, to remember, to keep the flame of her parents' love burning within her.

14
TIMOTHY

Annabelle's second winter at Thornfield Orphanage arrived with biting winds that howled through the cracks in the dormitory walls. The rhythm of orphanage life—the clanging bell, the cold gruel, the endless labour—had become as familiar to her as breathing, yet no less punishing. Her hands, once soft from tending her mother's roses, had grown calloused and chapped. The skin around her fingernails cracked and bled in the cold, but she no longer winced at the sting of lye soap.

She had learned to keep her head down and her thoughts private. The matrons valued silence and efficiency above all else, and Annabelle had become proficient at both. Yet beneath her quiet exterior, her mind remained alive with memories and questions, with snippets of her father's sermons and her mother's gentle wisdom.

At night, when the dormitory fell silent save for the occasional whimper or cough, Annabelle would carefully extract her father's Bible from its hiding place beneath a loose floorboard. The pages had begun to wear thin at the edges from her nightly readings, but the words still offered comfort—a reminder that she was more than just another nameless child in a grey uniform.

Still, there were moments when the loneliness threatened to overwhelm her. The other girls kept to themselves, too exhausted or too wary to form friendships. They moved through their days like ghosts, their eyes fixed on the floor, their spirits seemingly as grey as their dresses. Annabelle sometimes wondered if she looked the same to them—just another shadow passing through the cold halls of Thornfield.

One blustery afternoon, as Annabelle and the other children were set to gathering stones from the eastern field—a pointless task designed merely to keep them occupied—she noticed a boy she hadn't seen before. He was taller than most of the boys his age, with a shock of dark hair that refused to lie flat despite the strict orphanage grooming standards. As he bent to lift a particularly large stone, she saw his face clearly for the first time.

His eyes were what caught her attention—quick, dark, and alive with an intelligence that seemed at odds with their bleak surroundings. While the other children worked mechanically, this boy moved with purpose, his gaze darting about as if cataloguing everything around him.

As Mr Pullter barked orders from the edge of the field, the boy mimicked the master's pompous stance behind his back. The children nearest him stifled giggles, their shoulders shaking with suppressed laughter. Even from a distance, Annabelle could see the mischievous quirk of his mouth, the expressive arch of his eyebrows as he continued his silent performance.

Annabelle bit her lip to suppress her own smile as she watched the boy's antics. It had been so long since she'd seen anyone at Thornfield show such spirit. Mr Pullter's back remained turned as the boy continued his mimicry, adding an exaggerated waddle to his impression that nearly caused one small girl to burst into laughter.

A sharp whistle cut through the air. The boy immediately straightened, his face transforming into a mask of dutiful compliance. Mr Pullter spun around, his suspicious gaze sweeping across the children, who had all returned to their tasks with artificial diligence.

"You there, new boy! What's your name?" Mr Pullter's voice cracked like a whip.

"Timothy, sir." The boy's voice was steady, betraying none of his earlier mischief.

"Think yourself clever, do you?"

"No, sir. Just picking up stones, sir."

Annabelle held her breath, waiting for the inevitable punishment. Instead, Mr Pullter merely narrowed his eyes.

"I've got my eye on you, boy." He turned to address all the children. "Back inside, the lot of you. Storm's coming."

As they filed toward the orphanage, Annabelle found herself walking beside the boy called Timothy. Up close, she could see he was older than she'd first thought—perhaps twelve or thirteen.

"That was dangerous," she whispered, keeping her eyes forward.

Timothy glanced at her, surprise flickering across his face at being addressed directly. "Worth it though," he whispered back. "Did you see those smiles? Bet it was the first in weeks?"

Before Annabelle could respond, the matron's sharp voice called for silence. But as they entered the grim building, Timothy caught her eye once more and gave her the smallest of winks.

That night, as Annabelle read her father's Bible by a sliver of moonlight, she found herself lingering over Proverbs: "A merry heart doeth good like a medicine." Perhaps, she thought, closing the book carefully, there were different kinds of courage to be found at Thornfield after all.

15
A PUPIL

Annabelle sat in a secluded corner of the orphanage yard during the brief afternoon respite. The matrons allowed fifteen minutes of fresh air—though "fresh" hardly described the sooty atmosphere that hung over Thornfield like a shroud. Still, it was a reprieve from the endless indoor labour.

With practiced stealth, she slipped her father's Bible from beneath her apron. The familiar weight in her hands brought comfort as she quietly recited the Twenty-Third Psalm, her voice barely above a whisper.

"The Lord is my shepherd; I shall not want..."

"Sounds like that shepherd's got his work cut out for him round here."

Annabelle startled, nearly dropping the precious book. Timothy stood before her, his dark eyes dancing with amusement despite the perpetual hunger that hollowed his cheeks.

"You shouldn't sneak up on people," she whispered, hastily moving to conceal the Bible.

"Don't put it away on my account." Timothy settled beside

her on the rough stone bench. "I've been watching you. Every break, same corner, same book. Must be quite a tale."

"It's the Bible. My father's."

Timothy cocked his head. "The one about the giant and the boy with the sling? I heard that one from a street preacher once."

"David and Goliath," Annabelle confirmed, a smile tugging at her lips despite herself. "There are many stories. About courage and faith and—"

"People who had it worse than us?" Timothy grinned, the expression transforming his gaunt face.

Annabelle found herself laughing—a rusty, unfamiliar sound. "Some of them, yes."

Timothy leaned closer, his voice dropping lower. "What's it like? Reading, I mean. Must be like having magic at your fingertips."

"You can't read?" Annabelle asked, then immediately regretted her tone when she saw Timothy's shoulders stiffen.

"Never had the chance, did I? My father worked the mines till the day the shaft collapsed. After that, it was work or starve for us all." His fingers traced invisible patterns on the bench. "Always wanted to learn, though."

Annabelle studied him—the intelligence in his eyes, the quickness of his wit. She recognised in him the same hunger that kept her reading by moonlight, the same determination to find meaning beyond Thornfield's walls.

"I could teach you," she offered suddenly. "With this." She tapped the worn leather cover.

Timothy's eyes widened. "You'd do that? For me?"

"We'd have to be careful. Find moments when no one's watching."

"I'm good at not being seen when I don't want to be,"

Timothy said, a conspiratorial gleam in his eye. "When do we start?"

"Tomorrow," Annabelle whispered, feeling a spark of purpose ignite within her for the first time since arriving at Thornfield. "During the laundry sorting. The matron always dozes after lunch."

16
TOGETHER

Annabelle glanced nervously over her shoulder before sliding the Bible from its hiding place beneath her folded apron. The laundry sorting room smelled of lye and damp linen, but the matron's soft snores from the corner chair assured their temporary safety.

"Here," she whispered, opening to a page marked with a thread from her sleeve. "We'll start with something simple."

Timothy hunched closer, his shoulder pressing against hers as they huddled over the worn pages. His finger traced beneath the words as Annabelle guided him through each syllable.

"In the be-gin-ning," he stumbled, brow furrowed in concentration.

"Beginning," Annabelle corrected gently. "Try again."

"In the beginning, God created the Heavens and the earth." His face lit up as the sentence formed completely. "I did it!"

"Shh!" Annabelle cautioned, though she couldn't suppress her smile. "You're a quick learner."

"Got a good memory," Timothy tapped his temple. "Had to

remember everything Father told me about the mines—which tunnels were safe, which weren't."

Over the following weeks, their clandestine lessons continued. Timothy absorbed words with remarkable speed, his memory allowing him to recall entire verses after hearing them only once or twice.

"The Lord is my shepherd," Timothy recited during their fourth lesson, his voice gaining confidence. "I shall not want."

"Want means need," Annabelle explained.

Timothy snorted. "Then that's a lie, isn't it? We want for plenty here."

Rather than being shocked, Annabelle found herself stifling a laugh. "Perhaps it means something different. Like having what truly matters."

"Like this?" Timothy gestured between them. "Learning? Friendship?"

Annabelle nodded, something warm unfurling in her chest. "Exactly like this."

Their moments together transformed the grinding monotony of orphanage life. Timothy's quick wit made Annabelle laugh for the first time since her parents' deaths, while her patient teaching gave him the gift of words.

"My father died in the mines," Timothy confided one day as they scrubbed pots in the scullery. "Cave-in. I still hear the sounds sometimes, in my dreams."

Annabelle's hands stilled. "My mother had consumption. Father followed six months later."

"Broken heart?" Timothy asked softly.

"That's what the village said."

Timothy nodded, understanding in his eyes that required no further explanation. "Well, we're quite the pair then, aren't we?"

During the endless hours of labor, they developed silent

signals—a raised eyebrow, a subtle nod—creating their own language amidst the enforced silence. Timothy showed Annabelle how to position her body to ease the strain of scrubbing floors, while she taught him how to fold linens more efficiently.

"We'll survive this place," Timothy whispered during one lesson. "Together."

17
SMALL JOYS

Annabelle watched Timothy crouch beside the stone wall during their brief outdoor break. He glanced furtively at the yard master before waving her over.

"Look what I found," he whispered, uncurling his fingers to reveal a smooth pebble with bands of white running through its grey surface. "Reminds me of clouds moving across the sky."

Annabelle took the stone, turning it over in her palm. "It's beautiful."

"Keep it," Timothy said. "For when you can't see the real sky."

These small treasures became their secret currency. A dandelion seed head smuggled inside Timothy's sleeve. A robin's feather Annabelle discovered while beating carpets. Each item sparked whispered conversations about the world beyond Thornfield's walls.

"If you could go anywhere," Timothy asked one evening as they sorted potatoes in the kitchen, "where would it be?"

Annabelle considered this while checking for sprouts. "The

sea. Father once described Brighton—how the waves crash against the shore and seagulls soar overhead."

"I'd go to London," Timothy replied. "See the palace. Maybe steal the queen's crown."

"Timothy!" Annabelle gasped, but couldn't suppress her giggle.

He grinned. "Just imagine her face when she finds it missing."

During particularly grueling tasks, they invented silent games—counting how many times Mr. Pullter adjusted his waistcoat or wagering on which dormitory matron would fall asleep first during prayers.

One rainy afternoon, Timothy saved half his bread from lunch. During laundry sorting, he slipped it to Annabelle when she mentioned feeling lightheaded from hunger.

"You need it more," she protested.

"My father always said to share what little you have," he insisted. "Makes what's left taste better."

Their Bible lessons evolved into storytelling sessions. Timothy, though still learning to read, crafted elaborate tales inspired by scripture.

"And then Jonah told the whale, 'Your breath smells terrible! When's the last time you cleaned your teeth?'" Timothy whispered, mimicking an affronted expression.

Annabelle pressed her hand against her mouth to stifle her laughter. "That's not how it happened!"

"How do you know? Were you there?" His eyes danced with mischief.

When Matron Clarke berated Annabelle for a missed spot on the dormitory floor, forcing her to scrub the entire room again, Timothy appeared at dusk with a cluster of bluebells.

"Found them by the fence," he explained. "Thought you might need reminding there's still pretty things in the world."

The flowers withered by morning, but their effect lingered in Annabelle's heart. During the harshest days—when her hands cracked and bled from lye soap or when hunger gnawed at her insides—she would touch the cloud-streaked pebble in her pocket and remember Timothy's words.

18

RUMOURS OF THATCHWOOD MILL

Annabelle noticed the change first—how conversations between the girls would abruptly cease when the matrons approached, how names were whispered with fearful glances. "Thatchwood Mill," they said, voices dropping to barely audible murmurs.

She and Timothy were sorting linens when she first heard it properly. Two older girls, Martha and Jane, folded sheets nearby, unaware of Annabelle's attentive ears.

"Heard they took Emma there last week," Martha whispered. "Third girl this month."

Jane's hands trembled as she smoothed a pillowcase. "None ever write back, do they? My cousin went two years past. Not a word since."

"It's the machines," Martha continued, her voice tightening. "Spinning jennies that catch fingers and arms if you're not quick enough. Betsy from the parish said a girl lost three fingers her first day."

Annabelle's stomach twisted. She caught Timothy's eye across the room and saw he'd heard too.

Later, in the yard, they huddled by the wall, shoulders pressed together against the bitter wind.

"Is it true about Thatchwood?" Annabelle asked.

Timothy nodded grimly.

Each day brought new whispers. How the mill windows were barred to prevent escape. How the children there worked fourteen hours without rest, their bodies wasting to nothing on meagre rations. How some disappeared altogether, their names struck from records as though they'd never existed.

"Sarah told me they lock the doors at night," whispered a thin girl with a scarred cheek. "A fire broke out last spring and three girls couldn't get out."

The tales painted Thatchwood's owner, Mr Thatchwood, as a monster in human form. He'd stroll the mill floor, eyeing each girl like merchandise, his walking stick tapping against the floorboards as he selected his next victim.

"We can't let them send us there," Timothy said one evening as they huddled in the shadows of the yard. His face was pale in the fading light. "Promise we'll warn each other if we hear anything."

Annabelle clutched his hand, her father's Bible pressed between their palms. "I promise."

"If they try to take you," Timothy whispered fiercely, "I'll create such a distraction they'll forget all about it."

"And if they come for you, I'll hide you," Annabelle vowed, though she couldn't imagine where, in this prison of stone and rules.

19
LOOMING NIGHTMARE

Annabelle's heart pounded each time Mr Pullter's gaze lingered on her during morning inspection. Would today be the day he might announce her transfer to Thatchwood Mill? The fear followed her like a shadow, growing longer as each week passed.

"We need somewhere," Timothy whispered during their Bible lesson. "Somewhere they can't find us."

It took them three days to discover it—a forgotten corner behind the woodshed where the yard wall had partially crumbled, creating a small alcove hidden by overgrown brambles. They cleared just enough space for two small bodies to sit pressed together, the thorns providing a natural barrier against discovery.

"Our kingdom," Timothy declared the first time they squeezed into the space.

Annabelle smiled. "Our haven."

They reinforced their hideaway with discarded planks scavenged during yard work, arranging them to look like carelessly piled lumber. Inside, they lined the ground with stolen burlap sacks to keep the damp at bay. Annabelle brought her Bible, and Timothy contributed a stub of pencil he'd found in the scullery.

In their sanctuary, whispers flowed freely.

"When I leave here," Timothy said one grey afternoon, "I'll find work on the ships. Sail to America, perhaps."

Annabelle leaned against him, warming herself with his dreams. "I'd like to teach someday. Real lessons, not just reading."

"You'd be brilliant at it. The children would adore you."

"Would you write to me from America?" Annabelle asked.

Timothy's face clouded. "I'll need more lessons first."

"I'll teach you. We have time."

But time felt increasingly precious as rumours of Thatchwood Mill grew darker. Each day brought new whispered horrors—of children worked until they collapsed, of mysterious accidents, of the mill owner's wandering hands.

"Ellen's gone," a hollow-eyed girl named Mary informed them during breakfast. "Taken yesterday. She cried and fought so hard they had to drag her to the carriage."

That night, Annabelle heard muffled sobs from three different beds. The next morning, she noticed two girls praying fervently during morning chores, their lips moving in silent desperation.

Annabelle awoke before dawn with a nameless dread pressing against her chest. She'd dreamt of Thatchwood Mill—of great wooden teeth grinding children to dust. The dormitory was still dark, filled with the shallow breathing of exhausted girls.

She slipped from her bed and crept to the loose floorboard beneath which she kept her father's Bible. Her fingers trembled as she traced the familiar leather binding. Four years had passed since she'd arrived at Thornfield, yet sometimes the loss of her parents felt as fresh as yesterday.

"Strength, not fear," she whispered to herself, remembering her father's words.

20
YEARS GO BY

Annabelle's days at Thornfield blurred together, each one indistinguishable from the last, save for her moments with Timothy. What had begun as simple reading lessons had blossomed into something precious—a friendship that sustained her through the bleakest days of orphanage life.

Four winters had passed since they'd first spoken in the yard. Four winters of shared secrets, whispered dreams, and stolen moments of joy amidst the grinding routine of Thornfield. They'd grown taller, thinner perhaps, but their spirits remained unbroken.

Their chores and jobs had changed as they had grown older, but not any less grueling. Sometimes, Annabelle would be out in charge of inducted newcomers. It broke her heart to have to show children as young as four to their tiny beds. The worst times were when she would have to kneel down to one and explain to them that their parents weren't coming back.

Each morning, Annabelle would search for Timothy's face amongst the grey-clad boys across the dining hall. He'd catch her eye and pull an exaggerated expression—mimicking Mr Pullter's perpetual scowl or Matron Clarke's pinched disapproval—that would force Annabelle to stifle her laughter behind her hand. These small rebellions kept the darkness at bay.

"Look," Timothy whispered one afternoon as they sorted linens. He opened his palm to reveal a crust of bread he'd saved from breakfast. "The old dragon was watching you skip your portion this morning. Can't have you wasting away."

Annabelle's stomach growled at the sight. She'd given half her breakfast to little Sarah, whose persistent cough worried her. "We'll share it," she insisted, breaking the crust into two uneven pieces and pushing the larger towards Timothy.

He shook his head, pushing it back. "I nicked an extra potato at lunch."

Their secret strategies extended beyond food. When Annabelle struggled with the heavy buckets during floor-washing, Timothy would create diversions—dropping items or asking complicated questions that required the matron's full attention—allowing Annabelle precious moments to rest her aching arms.

During oakum picking, when Annabelle's fingers bled from separating the coarse rope fibres, Timothy would position himself to shield her from view, allowing her to work more slowly while he picked at double speed.

"Tell us about the ships again," she'd whisper during their Bible lessons, loving how Timothy's face transformed when he spoke of distant horizons.

"Magnificent vessels," he'd begin, eyes alight with dreams. "Tall as churches with sails that catch the wind like great white birds."

His clever tales weren't just for her benefit. Timothy had

developed a reputation among the guards as an amusing distraction. He'd spin elaborate stories that made even stern-faced Mr Jenkins chuckle, creating precious moments when vigilance slackened and tasks became bearable.

21
NIGHTTIME STORIES

Annabelle stood in the yard, hands raw from scrubbing floors, when the commotion at the gates drew her attention. A small cart rumbled through, carrying three girls who had been sent to Thatchwood Mill nearly a year prior. Annabelle recognised Ellen among them, though she might not have if not for the girl's distinctive mole near her left eye. The rest of her had changed beyond recognition.

"Look," Annabelle whispered to Timothy, who stood nearby sorting coal.

The girls descended from the cart with slow, mechanical movements. Their faces, once round with youth despite meagre rations, had hollowed to sharp angles and ashen skin. But it was their eyes that made Annabelle's heart clench—vacant and staring, as though something vital had been extinguished within them.

"They've come back for supplies," Timothy murmured, edging closer to Annabelle. "Heard Jenkins saying they needed more girls for the mill."

Ellen passed within arm's reach of Annabelle. Her hands

were wrapped in dirty bandages, fingers bent at unnatural angles. When Annabelle whispered her name, Ellen's gaze flickered briefly toward her, but no recognition dawned in those empty eyes.

"What happened to your hands?" Annabelle asked softly.

"Machine took three fingers," Ellen replied, voice flat as a winter field. "Mr Thatchwood says I'm lucky it wasn't more."

Annabelle fought the urge to reach for Timothy's hand as Ellen shuffled away.

Later, behind the woodshed in their secret place, Annabelle couldn't stop shaking. "Did you see them? Like ghosts walking about in girls' bodies."

Timothy nodded grimly. "We can't let them separate us, Belle. Whatever happens."

"We won't," Annabelle said, fierce conviction burning through her fear. She reached into her pocket and withdrew her father's Bible, its leather cover worn smooth from countless readings. "This kept me alive when I first came here. It's all I have of them—my parents. But it's more than just memories now."

She opened to where a pressed bluebell—Timothy's gift from years ago—marked her favourite passage.

"Let's make a promise," she said. "By this Bible and everything it means to us. We'll protect each other, no matter what comes."

Timothy placed his hand over the open pages. "I promise, Belle. Whatever happens, we face it together."

Annabelle laid her hand atop his. "Together."

That night, they slipped out to their haven beneath the stars. The spring air carried the scent of distant fields as they lay side by side, fingers intertwined.

"Tell me about the brave girl who spoke to birds," Timothy whispered.

Annabelle smiled, remembering her mother's stories. "She wasn't afraid of anything because she knew she was never truly alone.

"The brave girl knew her greatest strength was in the smallest of things," Annabelle continued, her voice barely above a whisper. "The birds taught her that even when storms came, they built their nests in places where the wind couldn't reach. So she did the same with her heart."

Timothy listened, his face tilted toward the stars. His breathing had slowed, and Annabelle knew he was drinking in every word as though it were water in this desert of a life.

"One day, when the girl felt most alone, a red-breasted robin landed on her windowsill. It sang to her about a garden where roses bloomed even in winter, where the sky never darkened, and where those we've lost wait for us with open arms."

Annabelle's voice caught. The story had been her mother's gift to her, and now it was hers to give to Timothy. In the telling, she felt her mother's presence so strongly it made her chest ache.

"Did she find the garden?" Timothy asked, his eyes reflecting pinpricks of starlight.

"Not yet," Annabelle said. "But the robin visits her every day, reminding her that it exists. And someday, when her work here is finished, she'll follow the robin there."

Timothy squeezed her hand. "I like that story."

"My mother told it to me," Annabelle said. "She said stories are like seeds—they grow inside us and give us strength when we need it most."

They fell silent, watching their breath form clouds in the chilly night air. The orphanage bell would ring soon, calling them back to their separate dormitories and another day of labour. But for now, in this moment, they had created a small pocket of freedom.

"We should go back," Annabelle said finally, though every part of her wanted to remain beneath the vast, indifferent sky.

Timothy nodded, reluctantly releasing her hand. "Tell me more tomorrow?"

"I promise," Annabelle said, tucking her father's Bible safely into her dress pocket. "There are many more stories to share."

22
THE LIST

Annabelle woke before the bell on her seventeenth birthday, her eyes tracing the familiar cracks in the dormitory ceiling. Seven years had passed since she first arrived at Thornfield, seven years since she'd last celebrated a birthday with cake or presents or anyone who truly cared other than Timothy. She dressed quickly in the grey uniform that hung loosely from her thin frame and tucked her father's Bible into its hiding place beneath her skirt.

The dining hall hummed with unusual tension that morning. Children huddled in tight clusters, their voices hushed, faces drawn with worry. Annabelle searched for Timothy among the sea of grey uniforms, finding him near the porridge vats. His eyes met hers across the room, and he gave her the smallest of nods—their private greeting.

"They're making a list," whispered Martha, sliding onto the bench beside Annabelle. "For the mill."

Annabelle's spoon froze halfway to her mouth. Every few months, Mr. Pullter selected girls for Thatchwood Mill, and they never returned the same—if they returned at all. She thought of Ellen's mangled hands, her vacant stare.

"It's your birthday, isn't it?" Timothy asked later, as they scrubbed the dining hall floors side by side. "Seventeen."

Annabelle nodded, memories washing over her—of her mother's garden, her father's study, Timothy's first reading lesson, the bluebell he'd given her that still was pressed between Bible pages. These small moments of grace had sustained her through seven years of hunger and cold and endless work.

"When we get out," Timothy said, voice low, "we'll have proper celebrations. With cake."

"And sea air," Annabelle added, allowing herself to imagine it. "Just like we planned."

The dining hall door crashed open. Mr Pullter strode in, ledger tucked beneath his arm, his thin lips pressed into a severe line. The scrubbing brushes stilled. Silence fell.

"Attention," he barked, unfolding a piece of paper. "The following girls have been selected for transfer to Thatchwood Mill, effective immediately."

A collective intake of breath rippled through the room. Annabelle's hands tightened around her brush, knuckles whitening.

"Margaret Lakes. Jane Ellis. Sarah Cooper."

Each name landed like a stone. Annabelle caught Timothy's gaze, his face tense with concern.

"Annabelle Sinclair."

The world tilted. Blood rushed in her ears as whispers erupted around her. She felt Timothy's hand brush against hers, but couldn't bring herself to look at him. Stories of the mill flooded her mind—the accidents, the locked doors, the cruel overseer. Her stomach clenched as she struggled to maintain composure, to not reveal the terror coursing through her veins.

Mr Pullter continued reading names, but Annabelle heard nothing more. Seven years of endurance, of small rebellions and secret lessons, of whispered stories and shared dreams—all to end at Thatchwood Mill, where girls returned broken if they returned at all.

23
A PLEA

Annabelle's legs trembled as she approached Mr. Pullter's office, her heart hammering against her ribs. The corridor stretched endlessly before her, each step bringing her closer to a fate she'd dreaded for years. She knocked on the door, her knuckles white against the dark wood.

"Enter," came the sharp command from within.

Mr Pullter sat behind his desk, not bothering to look up as she stepped inside. Sunlight slanted through the grimy window, illuminating dust motes that danced in the air between them.

"Mr Pullter, sir," Annabelle began, her voice barely above a whisper. She cleared her throat and tried again. "I've come about the transfer to Thatchwood Mill."

He glanced up, his expression blank. "What of it?"

"Please, sir, I—I believe there's been a mistake." The words tumbled out in a desperate rush. "I have family, sir. Distant cousins in Somerset who might take me in. And I've been teaching the younger children to read. I could be of use here, sir, truly I could."

Mr Pullter's pen scratched across paper, the sound unnervingly loud in the silence that followed.

"I've learned so much here," she continued, hating the tremor in her voice. "I could become a governess perhaps, or—"

"Enough." He set down his pen with deliberate slowness. "Your fantasies are of no concern to me, Miss Sinclair. My duty is to maintain order and efficiency in this institution."

"But sir—"

"Work at the mill is a privilege," he said, his tone suggesting it was anything but. "You should be grateful for the opportunity to contribute to society rather than remaining a burden."

Annabelle's throat tightened. The coldness in his eyes confirmed everything she'd feared—that she was nothing more than a name in his ledger, a problem to be managed.

"The carriage departs in one hour," he continued, already returning to his paperwork. "You are dismissed."

As the matron led her back to the dormitory, Annabelle lifted her chin. She would not break. Not here, not in front of them. The faces of the other girls selected for transfer reflected her own fear, but also a quiet determination. They nodded to one another, a silent acknowledgment of shared fate.

In the quiet of her mind, Annabelle heard Timothy's laugh, felt the warmth of his hand against hers as they shared stolen moments behind the woodshed. She recalled their whispered plans of freedom, of sea air and distant horizons. The memory steadied her. If she had survived seven years at Thornfield, she could survive whatever awaited her at Thatchwood Mill.

24
THE CARRIAGE

Annabelle returned to the dormitory, her steps measured despite the urgency pounding in her chest. Seven years of discipline had taught her to move without drawing attention, even as her mind raced with possibilities. She knelt beside her narrow cot and reached beneath it, fingers searching for the loose floorboard that had been her secret keeper all these years.

The wood gave way with practiced ease. Annabelle withdrew her father's Bible, its leather binding worn smooth from countless readings. She ran her fingertips over the gilt-edged pages, feeling the comforting weight of it in her hands. Inside lay pressed bluebells from Timothy, fragments of their shared history tucked between sacred pages.

She gathered her few possessions—a spare dress more patched than original fabric, a thin cotton nightdress, and a comb missing half its teeth. Everything fit into a small bundle that seemed a paltry sum for seventeen years of life. With deft movements born of necessity, she tucked the Bible beneath her shawl, close against her ribs where its presence steadied her racing heart.

The matron's voice cut through the dormitory. "Hurry along now! Carriages won't wait!"

Outside, the afternoon air hung heavy and still. Dark clouds massed overhead, casting the yard in gloomy shadows. Annabelle squinted upward, noting how the sky seemed to mirror the dread pooling in her stomach. The rumble of carriage wheels on gravel drew her attention to the gate where several conveyances waited.

A guard with weathered features gestured impatiently toward the last carriage. "In you go, girl. Quick about it."

"Wait..." Annabelle searched for Timothy. She had to say goodbye. She had to.

But he was nowhere to be seen.

Sarah, Martha and Jane already huddled inside, their faces pale ovals in the dimness. Annabelle climbed in, the wooden step creaking beneath her weight. As she settled onto the hard bench, the reality of her situation crashed over her. She was leaving—leaving Timothy, leaving the only place she'd known since her parents died, leaving for somewhere infinitely worse.

The carriage lurched forward. Annabelle clutched her bundle tightly against her chest, feeling the hard outline of the Bible press against her. The other girls stared at the floor or out the small windows, each lost in private misery. No one spoke. What was there to say when words could not change their destination?

Annabelle felt the walls of the carriage closing in with each turn of the wheels. The space between the girls seemed to shrink, though none of them had moved an inch. She pressed her father's Bible against her heart, its familiar weight a comfort against the hollow ache in her chest. The worn leather cover, smooth from years of handling, reminded her of evenings by the vicarage fire when Father's voice had brought the scriptures to life.

The other girls sat in stony silence. Jane's knuckles had gone white from gripping the edge of the bench. Sarah stared at her lap, her thin shoulders curved inward as if to make herself smaller. Martha's jaw was set tight, her eyes fixed on some distant point beyond the carriage window.

Annabelle drew in a deep breath, then another. The air inside the carriage was stale, but she focused on the rhythm of her breathing, using it to calm the storm of fear threatening to overwhelm her. Father's words echoed in her memory: "You have your mother's strength, Annabelle. Remember that when darkness seems to press in from all sides."

She had promised him she would remain brave, no matter what life threw at her. That promise now felt like a lifeline in a churning sea.

The carriage bumped along the rutted road, jostling its occupants with each hole and stone. Annabelle turned her gaze to the small window, watching as familiar countryside gave way to unknown terrain. Rolling hills dotted with sheep faded into thicker woods, the trees pressing close to the road like silent sentinels. How different this journey was from the one that had brought her to Thornfield seven years ago.

Images of Thatchwood Mill formed in her mind—a hulking building of brick and smoke, windows barred to keep children in rather than danger out. She remembered Ellen's vacant stare, her mangled fingers, and the way she flinched at sudden movements. Was that to be Annabelle's fate as well?

No. She would not surrender to despair. She and Timothy had whispered dreams of freedom behind the woodshed—dreams of teaching for her, of sailing to America for him. Those dreams still lived, even if Timothy was not beside her now.

Annabelle clutched the Bible tighter, her thumb finding the

familiar crack in its spine where she had so often opened to Psalms. "The Lord is my light and my salvation; whom shall I fear?" she whispered, too softly for the others to hear. The words settled into her bones, kindling a small flame of determination. Whatever awaited her at Thatchwood Mill, she would face it standing tall.

25
FREEDOM

Annabelle pressed her face against the small window as the carriage picked up speed, lurching over a pothole. Then suddenly—a violent jolt threw all four girls forward. Annabelle's head nearly struck the opposite wall as the vehicle skidded and came to an abrupt halt.

The carriage lurched again as one of the wheels creaked, and Annabelle thought it sounded like somebody clambering up on top of the roof.

The driver's cry of surprise rang out, followed by the sound of scrambling feet and a dull thud.

Sarah whimpered. Martha clutched Jane's arm. Annabelle leaned toward the window, straining to see what had happened, but the angle revealed nothing but empty road.

"What's happening?" whispered Jane, her voice thin with fear.

Before anyone could answer, the carriage door flew open with such force it bounced against the outer panel. Jane screamed, recoiling against the back of the carriage.

Annabelle's heart stopped.

Timothy stood there, chest heaving, his wild eyes meeting hers. His uniform was smeared with dirt, his face flushed with exertion. Strands of dark hair plastered to his forehead with sweat. The sight of him sent a shock through Annabelle's body—equal parts disbelief and desperate hope.

He glanced over his shoulder, then jerked his head toward something on the ground. Annabelle leaned forward to see the driver sprawled in the dirt, motionless.

Timothy's familiar grin flashed across his face, mischievous and urgent. Sweat dripped from his brow as he extended his hand toward her, his eyes never leaving hers.

"Fancy a walk?" he asked, grinning as he held out his hand towards Annabelle.

Without a moment's hesitation, she grabbed Timothy's outstretched hand. The moment their fingers touched, something electric shot through her—a spark of connection, of shared purpose that ignited every instinct to flee. Her father's Bible clutched tightly against her chest, she leapt from the carriage, her feet striking the packed dirt road with a jolt that travelled up her legs.

"Run!" Timothy shouted to the other girls. "Go on, all of you!"

Jane, Martha and Sarah scrambled out behind them, wide-eyed and trembling. They exchanged no words of gratitude, no backward glances—just fled in the opposite direction, their grey dresses soon disappearing around a bend in the road.

The driver lay motionless nearby, a rock clutched in Timothy's free hand explaining his condition. Timothy tossed it aside and tugged Annabelle toward the dense woods lining the roadside.

"Come on!" he urged, his fingers tightening around hers.

Together they sprinted across the open ground, Annabelle's lungs burning as they reached the first line of trees. The thrill of liberation surged through her veins, drowning out the voice of caution that had governed her years at Thornfield. Behind them, a cloud of dust from the road marked all they were leaving behind—the orphanage, the daily humiliations, and the looming threat of Thatchwood Mill.

Cool air enveloped them as they weaved between ancient oaks and tangled underbrush. Branches whipped past Annabelle's face, catching at her skirt and hair, but she pushed forward, matching Timothy's pace. Their breath came in quick, desperate gasps as they plunged deeper into the protective embrace of the forest.

"Did you—" Annabelle panted, ducking beneath a low-hanging branch, "—did you plan this?"

Timothy's laugh burst forth, wild and untamed. "Half-planned! Saw them taking you this morning. I hid in the one place they wouldn't look. I stowed away under the carriage!"

"You held onto the carriage for that long?" Annabelle asked in disbelief.

"Of course!" Timothy said. "I couldn't let them—"

He didn't finish the sentence. He didn't need to.

Annabelle's heart raced, keeping time with Timothy's quick footsteps beside her. A breathless laugh escaped her lips, mingling with the rustling leaves overhead. It was madness—pure, exhilarating madness. They were fugitives now, but they were free.

26

ANOTHER LOSS

Annabelle's legs ached with each step, yet she pressed forward through the darkness, Timothy's hand still firmly clasped in hers. The rhythm of their flight had slowed from a desperate sprint to a steady march, their bodies demanding respite even as their minds urged them onward.

The first hint of dawn appeared as a faint glow on the horizon, transforming the menacing shadows of night into the soft outlines of trees. Annabelle watched the gradual lightening of the sky with wonder. How different this sunrise felt from the hundreds she had witnessed at Thornfield, where morning light merely heralded another day of drudgery. This dawn marked something else entirely—a boundary between captivity and possibility.

"Look," she whispered, nodding toward the east where pink tendrils stretched across the sky. "We've survived the night."

Timothy squeezed her hand in response, his face haggard but determined. They had spoken little during their journey, saving their breath for the endless walking, but the shared silence carried its own comfort.

The woods thinned slightly as they crested a small rise. Brambles caught at Annabelle's skirt, tearing small holes in the coarse grey fabric. She found she didn't care. The orphanage uniform would need to be discarded soon anyway—it marked them too clearly as fugitives.

"Need to rest," Timothy murmured, his voice rough with fatigue. "Just for a moment."

Annabelle nodded, her own exhaustion bone-deep. They had pushed themselves through the night, fear and exhilaration propelling them forward, but their bodies could not sustain such effort indefinitely.

The shepherd's hut appeared so suddenly that Annabelle thought she might be dreaming—a small, weathered structure nestled against the side of a hill, its stone walls blending with the landscape. Timothy spotted it at the same moment, his pace quickening despite his exhaustion.

"There," he pointed. "Shelter."

They approached cautiously, Timothy circling the structure once to ensure it was truly abandoned before pushing open the creaking wooden door. Inside, the hut was sparse but dry—a dirt floor, stone walls, and a small hearth long cold. Cobwebs hung from the low ceiling, and the musty scent of disuse filled the space.

Annabelle stepped inside, her legs finally giving way as she slid down against the rough wall. Timothy collapsed beside her, their shoulders touching as they both struggled to catch their breath.

The faint light of dawn filtered through gaps in the wooden door, casting strips of gold across the earthen floor. Annabelle turned to Timothy, meeting his gaze. His face was smudged with dirt, his eyes red-rimmed with fatigue, yet they shone with the same wild hope that thrummed through her own veins.

"We did it," she whispered, clutching her father's Bible to her chest. "We actually escaped."

Annabelle gazed around the shepherd's hut, reality settling over her like a heavy cloak. The exhilaration of escape gradually yielded to the weight of their circumstances. Fugitives. The word hung unspoken between them, carrying implications neither had fully considered in their desperate flight.

"They'll be looking for us," she said quietly, tracing her finger along the worn leather cover of her father's Bible. "Two youths travelling together will draw attention."

Timothy nodded, his expression solemn. "I've been thinking the same. We'd be remembered. Two runaways stick in people's minds."

The truth of his words pierced her heart. Annabelle had imagined their freedom would mean staying together, protecting one another as they always had. Now, the cruel reality of their situation demanded otherwise.

"We'll need to separate," Timothy said, voicing the thought she couldn't bring herself to speak. "It's the only way."

Annabelle felt tears prick at her eyes but refused to let them fall. "I know," she whispered. "I just didn't think our freedom would begin with another loss."

Timothy shifted, taking both her hands in his. His palms were rough from years of labour, familiar and comforting against her own calloused skin.

"I'm heading north to Liverpool," he said. "There's work on the docks there—I heard the warden talking about it once. Men are always needed to load ships."

Annabelle nodded, trying to imagine Timothy among sailors and dockhands, his quick mind and strong back serving him well in that new world.

"And you?" Timothy asked, his voice catching slightly. "Where will you go?"

"East," she replied, the decision forming even as she spoke it. "Perhaps I can find work as a governess or a teacher's assistant. Father always said I had a gift for explaining things."

The silence that followed felt unbearable. Seven years of friendship, of shared hardships and stolen moments of joy, now culminating in this painful farewell.

"I'll find you again," Timothy said fiercely. "Once I've made something of myself. I promise."

"And I'll be looking for you," Annabelle replied, her voice steady despite the storm inside her. "We've survived Thornfield. We can survive this too."

Timothy's eyes glistened as he squeezed her hands one last time. "Your father was right, you know. You do have your mother's strength."

Annabelle clutched her Bible tighter, the only physical connection to her past. "And you have courage enough for both of us."

27
UNTIL WE MEET AGAIN

The sun rose fully now, casting dappled golden light through the forest canopy. Dust motes danced in the beams that streamed through the hut's open door. The time had come. Annabelle felt her heart constrict.

Timothy stood before her, his familiar face etched with the same pain she felt. Seven years of friendship, of whispered stories and shared burdens, of small kindnesses that had kept them both alive through the grinding misery of Thornfield. And now, they must part.

"This isn't goodbye," Timothy said, his voice rough. "Just... until we meet again."

Annabelle nodded, unable to speak past the lump in her throat. They moved toward each other simultaneously, arms encircling in one final embrace. She breathed in his scent—soap and sweat and something uniquely Timothy—committing it to memory. His arms tightened around her, warm and solid, a final shelter before the cold uncertainty that awaited them both.

"Be careful," she whispered against his shoulder. "Don't let anyone see the real you until you know they can be trusted."

"Same to you," he murmured into her hair. "Keep that clever mind hidden until you're safe."

They released each other reluctantly, fingers lingering on sleeves, neither wanting to be the first to step away. But they must. For survival. For freedom.

Annabelle clutched her Bible to her chest, its familiar weight anchoring her to the past even as she prepared to step into an unknown future. She moved to the doorway, pausing to look back at Timothy one last time. His figure stood silhouetted against the dim interior of the hut, tall and lean, his expression a mixture of sorrow and determination.

Taking a deep breath, Annabelle stepped out into the early morning light. The forest air felt different somehow—fresher, wilder, tinged with possibility and danger in equal measure. She adjusted her shawl, squared her shoulders, and began walking eastward, each step carrying her further from everything familiar.

The woods gradually thickened around her, branches reaching overhead like cathedral arches. Birds called to one another in the canopy, oblivious to the small figure moving beneath them. Annabelle forged ahead, her feet finding a steady rhythm on the forest floor. Each step resonated with a peculiar mixture of hope and fear—the terrifying freedom of being entirely on her own for the first time in her life.

28

A LONG WALK

The gentle roll of hills stretched out before Annabelle, a patchwork of emerald fields dotted with wildflowers that swayed in the afternoon breeze. Sunlight bathed the landscape in golden warmth, casting long shadows across the countryside. In the distance, a cluster of thatched roofs nestled against the horizon, smoke rising from chimneys in lazy spirals.

Annabelle stumbled forward, her legs trembling beneath her threadbare skirt. Three days of walking had left her feet blistered and raw, each step a fresh torment. Her blouse was smudged with dirt, her copper curls matted against her hollow cheeks. The beautiful vista before her blurred as she blinked away exhaustion.

Her stomach twisted painfully, a constant reminder of how long it had been since she'd eaten anything more substantial than a handful of berries scavenged from roadside bushes. Water from streams had sustained her, but hunger clawed at her insides like a living thing.

"Just a bit further," she whispered to herself, her voice cracked and thin.

The distant village beckoned, stirring fragments of memory—market days with Father, his hand warm around hers as they'd travelled to purchase books. Had they passed through here? The shapes of the buildings seemed vaguely familiar, yet everything blurred together in her weary mind.

Her thoughts drifted to Timothy. Was he safe? Would he safely reach Liverpool? The memory of his face, determined yet frightened as they'd parted ways, sent a fresh wave of loneliness washing over her. Their promise to find each other again someday felt impossibly distant now.

"We'll meet again," she murmured, clutching her father's Bible closer to her chest. "We must."

The weight of solitude pressed down upon her shoulders more heavily than her physical exhaustion. For six years, Timothy had been her constant companion, her brother in all but blood. Without him beside her, the world seemed vaster and more threatening.

Annabelle forced herself onward, past a cluster of oak trees whose branches swayed gently overhead. The village was closer now, but the distance seemed to stretch impossibly before her failing strength.

Her vision swam, dark spots dancing at the edges. She stumbled, her knees buckling beneath her. The Bible slipped from her grasp as she collapsed into the tall grass, its pages fluttering open beside her.

The last thing Annabelle saw was a butterfly landing on a nearby dandelion, its wings a brilliant blue like the bluebells Timothy had once pressed between the pages of her father's Bible. Then darkness claimed her, the sounds of birds and rustling leaves fading into silence.

29
JACOB BENNETT

Jacob Bennett trudged along the edge of his wheat field, inspecting the new growth with satisfaction. The morning dew dampened his boots as he walked the perimeter, planning the day's work in his mind. The eastern boundary of his land stretched toward the old coach road, and as he reached the far corner, something caught his eye—an unusual shape disturbing the even sway of the tall grass.

He squinted against the morning sun. A bundle of cloth, perhaps? No—the shape was too distinct. A small figure lay crumpled at the field's edge.

"What..." he muttered, quickening his pace. His weathered hands pushed aside the tall grass as he approached. It was a girl, hardly more than a child, face-down in the grass with one arm outstretched toward a worn book.

Jacob knelt beside her, noticing her thin frame and tattered clothes. Her copper hair spilled across the grass like copper wire.

"Miss? Can you hear me?" He placed a gentle hand on her

shoulder, giving it a slight shake. "Come now, lass, open your eyes."

The girl remained still. Jacob's heart quickened. He pressed two fingers against her neck, relieved to find a pulse, though faint.

"There we are, still with us," he murmured. "Let's get you some help."

Her eyelids fluttered open, revealing startling blue eyes that widened with fear before clouding with confusion.

"You're all right now," Jacob said, his voice softening. "I've got you."

The girl's lips moved, but no sound emerged. Her skin felt cold to the touch, and Jacob noticed the angry blisters on her feet, the hollowness of her cheeks. She'd been walking for days, he reckoned, and without proper food.

He scooped up the book—a Bible—and tucked it into his coat. With practiced ease, he gathered the girl into his arms. She weighed no more than his youngest child.

"Help!" he called, striding toward the village, his voice carrying across the morning stillness. "Dr Miller! Someone fetch the doctor!"

Villagers emerged from their cottages as Jacob hurried down the main street, the girl's head lolling against his shoulder.

"What's happened, Bennett?" called the blacksmith, stepping from his forge.

"Found her collapsed in my field," Jacob replied without slowing. "She needs the doctor, quick!"

Mrs Hadley, the baker's wife, rushed ahead to knock on the doctor's door while Jacob followed, cradling the girl against his chest. Dr Miller appeared moments later, ushering them inside.

"Here, on the table," the doctor instructed, clearing space on his examination table.

Jacob laid her down with care, supporting her head until it rested on the worn leather surface.

"She's half-starved, Doctor," Jacob said, stepping back. "Found her just lying there with nothing but this Bible." He pulled the book from his coat.

Jacob watched Dr Miller tend to the girl with practiced movements. The doctor's hands, usually steady during even the most difficult births, showed unusual gentleness as he cleaned the dirt from her face with a damp cloth.

"She's been on the road for days, I'd wager," Dr Miller said, examining her blistered feet. "Severe exhaustion, dehydration. Lucky you found her when you did, Bennett."

Jacob nodded, clutching the girl's Bible in his weathered hands. The leather binding was worn smooth at the edges, the pages yellowed with age and use. Not the sort of possession one would expect from a vagrant child.

"Will she recover?" Jacob asked, thinking of his own children safe at home.

"With proper care, yes." The doctor reached for a bottle of tonic. "Mary!" he called to his housekeeper. "Bring broth and bread, quickly now."

The girl's eyes fluttered open again, more alert this time. She tried to sit up, panic flashing across her face.

"Easy there," Jacob said, stepping closer. "You're safe, miss. I'm Jacob Bennett. Found you at the edge of my field."

She glanced between the two men, then at the door, as if calculating an escape. Her hand moved instinctively to her side, searching.

"Looking for this?" Jacob held out the Bible. "It's safe. I kept it for you."

Relief washed over her face as she took the book, clutching it to her chest like a shield.

"What's your name, child?" Dr Miller asked, helping her sit up against the pillows.

She hesitated, eyes darting between them. "Annabelle," she finally whispered, her voice hoarse.

Mary entered with a tray of steaming broth and fresh bread. The girl—Annabelle—eyed it with poorly concealed hunger.

"Slowly now," Dr Miller cautioned as she reached for the spoon with trembling fingers.

Jacob shifted his weight, uncomfortable in the small room. "Where are you headed, Annabelle? Do you have family waiting?"

She paused mid-sip, wariness returning to her eyes. "I... I don't know if..."

"Rest now," Jacob said, nodding respectfully. "Meadowbrook's a good village. When you're stronger, perhaps we can help you find what you're looking for."

30
UNTOLD STORY

Annabelle woke to sunlight streaming through unfamiliar curtains. For a fleeting moment, panic seized her chest before she remembered—she had escaped. The orphanage walls no longer imprisoned her, though the memories remained etched in her mind like carvings on stone.

A man she didn't know entered the room. Wait, no... He was the doctor. "Good morning, Annabelle. I'm Doctor Miller. How are we feeling today?"

"Better, thank you," Annabelle replied, her voice still rough from disuse.

She sat up slowly, and a groan escaped her as she felt how stiff all her muscles were.

"You've been on the road a long time I would guess." The doctor said gently.

Annabelle nodded, picking up and tracing the worn leather of her father's Bible. The familiar weight in her hands transported her back to the vicarage, to evenings by the fire with Mother's laughter filling the room. She opened to Psalms, reading her father's annotations in the margins, his neat script a comfort across time and distance.

"The Lord is my shepherd; I shall not want," she whispered, fingers tracing the words. Timothy would be walking toward Liverpool now, perhaps already finding work at the docks. The thought of him facing the world alone twisted her heart.

"Your colour's returning," Dr Miller observed the next morning while checking her pulse. "You gave poor Jacob quite a fright, collapsing at the edge of his field."

"I'm sorry for the trouble," Annabelle replied, eyes downcast.

"No trouble at all. Though I wonder what brings a young woman your age to travel alone through the countryside."

Annabelle's fingers twisted in the blanket. "I'm seeking employment as a governess or teacher's assistant. I've always had a way with children."

"And your family? Surely they worry for you."

"They've passed on," she said simply, the truth easier than fabrication.

Dr Miller's eyes softened. "I see you keep this Bible close. Your father's?"

"It's all I have of him now."

"Miss Annabelle," he said gently, settling into the chair beside her bed, "I've treated enough patients to know when someone is running from something. I could help you better if you'd share your story."

Annabelle met his gaze, measuring her response. "You've already shown me great kindness, Dr Miller. Some stories are better left untold, at least for now. Please understand."

She offered a smile that didn't quite reach her eyes, grateful when he nodded and changed the subject to her recovery instead.

31
HARRIET CHILTON

Harriet Chilton wove her way through Meadowbrook's bustling market square, her leather satchel swinging against her hip as she navigated between stalls laden with spring produce. The morning air buzzed with conversation, and for once, it wasn't about Mrs Fallington's new hat or Farmer Wilkes's prize pig.

"They say she speaks like a lady," Mrs Cooper whispered to Mrs Jennings at the baker's stall, "yet she arrived with naught but the clothes on her back and that old Bible."

"Dr Miller claims she's recovering well," replied Mrs Jennings, lowering her voice as Harriet approached. "Good morning, Miss Chilton!"

Harriet nodded politely, pretending not to have overheard, though her ears had pricked up at the mention of the mysterious girl who'd collapsed on the outskirts of their village three days prior.

"I heard she can read," piped up young Billy Cooper, his mother's shopping basket clutched in his grubby hands. "Read proper books too, not just picture ones."

Harriet paused at the vegetable stall, selecting carrots while listening intently. The village had been abuzz with speculation since Jacob Bennett had carried the unconscious girl to Dr Miller's surgery. Some whispered she was a runaway servant, others suggested a governess fallen on hard times. What intrigued Harriet most was the consistent mention of the girl's refined speech and apparent education.

"Poor thing," muttered Mr Timms, the butcher, wrapping a cut of lamb for the vicar's housekeeper. "Thin as a rake, she is. Whatever she's running from must be worse than starving in a ditch."

Harriet's hand stilled over a bunch of spring onions. In her fifteen years as Meadowbrook's schoolmistress, she'd developed an instinct for children in need. Though by all accounts, this Annabelle wasn't precisely a child, something about her story tugged at Harriet's heart.

"Begging your pardon, Miss Chilton," called Mrs Finchly from behind her ribbon stall, "but aren't you looking for a helper at the school? Perhaps this newcomer might suit?"

Harriet smiled, not surprised that Mrs Finchly had read her thoughts. "Perhaps indeed," she replied, handing over coins for her vegetables. "I believe I shall pay Dr Miller a visit this afternoon."

Decision made, Harriet quickened her steps through the market. Her cottage could wait; the school lessons were prepared for tomorrow. Right now, her curiosity about this well-spoken young woman with nothing but a Bible to her name simply couldn't be contained.

Harriet arrived at Dr Miller's modest office, its whitewashed walls and green door a familiar sight to all in Meadowbrook. She smoothed her skirt before knocking, suddenly aware she hadn't planned her approach beyond satisfying her curiosity.

Dr Miller himself answered, spectacles perched on his nose and sleeves rolled to the elbow.

"Miss Chilton! What a pleasant surprise. Nothing amiss at the school, I hope?"

"Nothing at all, Dr Miller. The children are in fine health, thank goodness." Harriet clutched her satchel a touch tighter. "I've come about... well, about your patient. The young woman Mr Bennett found."

Dr Miller's eyebrows rose slightly. "Ah, I see the village grapevine functions as efficiently as ever."

"Indeed." Harriet felt a flush creep into her cheeks. "I confess I'm curious. They say she's educated, and I wondered if perhaps..."

"If perhaps you might help?" Dr Miller's expression softened. "Come in, then. She's much improved, though still weak. Quite the mystery, our Annabelle."

He led Harriet through the narrow hallway, past his surgery room with its distinct medicinal smell, and toward the back of the house.

"She's in here," he murmured, gesturing to a door left slightly ajar. "Barely spoken two words together about where she's from or where she's headed. But perhaps you'll have better luck."

Dr Miller pushed the door open gently and stepped aside. "I'll bring tea shortly."

Harriet nodded her thanks and moved into the small guest room. The curtains were drawn halfway, allowing a shaft of afternoon sunlight to spill across the simple bed and wooden chair beside it.

The bed was empty, but in the corner of the room, nestled in the window seat, sat a slender figure. Annabelle had drawn her knees up, creating a makeshift lectern for the worn leather Bible open in her lap. Her copper curls caught the sunlight, forming a copper halo around her downturned face. Her lips moved silently as her finger traced along the lines of text.

Harriet paused, reluctant to disturb the scene. There was something deeply moving about the girl's absorption in the text—a reverence that reminded Harriet of her own father, who had been a devout man. The young woman's brow furrowed in concentration, then smoothed as her lips curved into a slight smile, as though she'd found precisely the passage she sought.

Harriet remained still, struck by the tableau before her—this mysterious girl who'd arrived with nothing, finding evident solace in ancient words.

32
CONFESSION

Annabelle's fingers traced the familiar verse in her father's Bible. She glanced up, and was startled from her reverie. A woman stood in the doorway—not the bustling Mary who'd brought broth earlier, nor Dr Miller with his kindly but probing questions.

This visitor wore a modest navy dress with a white collar, her dark brown hair swept into a neat bun that revealed an oval face with intelligent hazel eyes. Something in her bearing—a quiet confidence, perhaps—reminded Annabelle of her mother.

"Good afternoon," the woman said, her voice gentle yet assured. "You must be Annabelle. I'm Miss Harriet Chilton, the schoolmistress here in Meadowbrook."

Annabelle closed her Bible, thumb marking her place. "Good afternoon, Miss Chilton."

The schoolmistress approached, her gaze falling to the worn Bible in Annabelle's hands. "Dr Miller mentioned you're quite fond of reading. That's a well-loved book you have there."

"It was my father's," Annabelle replied, her fingers brushing the leather binding. "He taught me to read from it."

Miss Chilton settled onto the chair beside the window seat. "And what were you reading just now?"

Annabelle hesitated, weighing caution against the relief of genuine conversation after years of whispers at Thornfield. "Ecclesiastes 'To everything there is a season, and a time to every purpose under heaven.'"

"A complex book for someone your age," Miss Chilton remarked, her eyebrows lifting slightly.

"Father said understanding comes not from age but from seeking." Annabelle opened the Bible again, revealing her father's neat annotations in the margins. "He believed Ecclesiastes teaches us about finding meaning in life's cycles—that joy and sorrow both have their place in shaping who we become."

Miss Chilton leant forward, her eyes brightening. "That's a remarkably thoughtful interpretation."

"Father and I would discuss such things during our evening readings." Annabelle traced one of her father's notes with her fingertip. "He said wisdom begins when we question not just what the words say, but what they mean for how we live."

"Your father sounds like he was a learned man."

"He was the vicar at St Michael's parish in Somerset," Annabelle said, the words slipping out before she could stop them.

Annabelle's heart lurched as the words left her mouth. What had she done?

"Please," Annabelle whispered, leaning forward urgently. "You mustn't tell anyone who I am. I—I shouldn't have said that."

Miss Chilton's expression shifted, concern replacing curiosity. "Why would that be a secret worth keeping, child?"

Annabelle glanced toward the door, then back to Miss Chilton. The woman's eyes held no judgment, only a steady patience that reminded her painfully of Father. Perhaps this was her one chance at a new beginning.

"After my parents died, the new vicar, Reverend Bloom, sent me to Thornfield Orphanage." The words tumbled out in a desperate rush. "He said there was nowhere else..."

Miss Chilton's brow furrowed. "You ran away from the orphanage?"

"I know it's wrong to disobey my elders," Annabelle said, her voice trembling. "The Bible teaches obedience, but it also speaks of justice. What they did wasn't just. And then they were going to send me to Thatchwood Mill." She shuddered. "Girls who go there come back broken—if they come back at all."

Annabelle's fingers traced the edge of her Bible, finding the place where Timothy's pressed bluebell remained hidden. "I couldn't stay. I couldn't go to the mill. So when there was a chance to escape, I took it."

She looked up at Miss Chilton, eyes brimming with unshed tears. "I know I've sinned in running away. But I also know that staying would have been a slow death of spirit, if not of body. Father always said God gives us wisdom to discern right from wrong, even when choices aren't simple.

"Please," Annabelle whispered. "Please don't send me back there."

Miss Chilton reached forward and placed her hand gently over Annabelle's. "Your secret is safe with me."

Relief flooded through Annabelle, leaving her light-headed. She hadn't realised how tightly she'd been holding herself until that moment.

Miss Chilton tilted her head, studying Annabelle with new interest. "You know, I have a young student— Thomas Fletcher. Bright as a new penny, but he simply cannot grasp his letters properly. We've tried everything, but the poor boy becomes so frustrated he often ends up in tears."

Annabelle nodded, recalling how Timothy had struggled with certain sounds when they'd first begun their lessons.

"Would you—" Miss Chilton paused, then continued with sudden decisiveness. "Would you be willing to sit with him? Perhaps this time tomorrow? I wonder if a fresh approach might help him."

The request caught Annabelle by surprise. Her? Teaching a child from the village? The thought was both thrilling and terrifying. What if she failed? What if the boy disliked her? What if his parents objected to a stranger instructing their son?

Yet beneath these worries flickered a small, bright flame of hope. This was what she'd dreamed of during those long nights at Thornfield—the chance to share knowledge rather than scrub floors until her hands bled.

"I would be honoured," Annabelle said, even as doubt gnawed at her. What did she know of proper teaching? Her lessons with Timothy had been conducted in whispers behind the laundry room, with only her father's Bible as a text.

But she remembered how Timothy's eyes had lit up the first time he'd read a full verse on his own. Perhaps she could bring that same joy to this boy.

"Excellent," Miss Chilton said, rising to her feet. "I'll make arrangements with Dr Miller. If you're feeling strong enough, we can try this tomorrow."

33
THE OFFER

The next afternoon Annabelle followed Miss Chilton through the village, her heart fluttering like a trapped bird. The schoolhouse stood at the edge of Meadowbrook—a modest building with a slate roof and windows that caught the afternoon light. Far grander than the orphanage, yet humbler than St Michael's parish school where Father had occasionally taught.

Miss Chilton pushed open the heavy wooden door. "Thomas is waiting inside. His mother brings him for extra lessons three times a week."

The classroom smelled of chalk dust and polish. A small boy sat hunched over a primer, his shoulders tense with frustration. Ink stained his fingers, and a crumpled paper lay discarded beside him.

"Thomas, I've brought someone to help with your reading today," Miss Chilton said.

The boy looked up, wariness etched across his freckled face. Annabelle recognised that expression—the same one Timothy had worn when she first offered to teach him.

Annabelle approached slowly, kneeling beside his chair until their eyes met. "Hello, Thomas. My name is Annabelle."

"Tommy," he corrected, his voice barely audible. "Everyone calls me Tommy."

"Tommy, then." Annabelle smiled. "Would you show me what you're reading?"

He pushed the book toward her reluctantly. Annabelle glanced at the page—a simple passage about a merchant and his wares.

"This looks interesting," she said, her voice gentle. "Shall we read it together?"

Tommy shrugged, but his eyes remained fixed on her face.

Annabelle began reading, her voice clear yet soft. She ran her finger beneath each word, pausing at natural breaks rather than rushing through. When she reached a difficult word, she broke it into smaller parts.

"Mer-chan-dise," she sounded out. "Do you know what that means, Tommy?"

He shook his head.

"It's all the things a merchant sells. Like at the market—the apples and bread and cloth. Those are his merchandise."

Tommy's brow furrowed in concentration. "Mer-chan-dise," he repeated carefully.

"That's it exactly!" Annabelle beamed. "Now, what do you think happens next in our story?"

As they continued reading, Tommy leaned closer. When they reached the end of the page, Annabelle asked him to try the next sentence alone. He hesitated, then began, stumbling only twice.

"You've done it!" Annabelle clapped her hands. "You read that beautifully."

Tommy's face transformed, pride replacing frustration as

comprehension dawned. "I did it," he whispered, amazement in his voice.

Across the room, Miss Chilton watched, her eyes bright with approval. The classroom, previously heavy with Tommy's frustration, now hummed with possibility. Annabelle felt it too—this moment of connection, of knowledge shared and received with joy rather than fear.

Tommy clutched his book to his chest as his mother arrived, a woman with work-worn hands and tired eyes that brightened when Miss Chilton described her son's progress. After they departed, Annabelle stood by the window, watching them cross the village green, Tommy chattering animatedly, pointing back at the schoolhouse.

"You have a remarkable gift," Miss Chilton said, joining her at the window. "Tommy has struggled for months with those passages. His father insists reading is a waste for a boy destined for farm work, but that child has a quick mind."

Annabelle felt warmth spread through her chest. "He simply needed patience. Sometimes children believe they cannot learn because they've been told as much."

Miss Chilton studied her with thoughtful eyes. "That's precisely it. You understand what many teachers never grasp—that belief shapes ability." She began tidying the classroom, straightening books with practiced movements. "Where did you learn to teach with such compassion?"

"My father," Annabelle replied, then hesitated. "And later... a friend at Thornfield. I taught him to read using my father's Bible."

"I see it in how you break words into manageable pieces, in your patience." Miss Chilton placed the last book on the shelf. "Annabelle, I've been struggling to manage the school alone since my assistant left to marry. The younger children particularly need individual attention."

Annabelle's hands stilled on the slate she'd been wiping clean.

"I'd like to offer you a position as my assistant," Miss Chilton continued. "You'd help with the younger students, particularly those struggling with their letters. I can provide a small stipend and a room in my cottage."

The offer hung in the air between them. Annabelle's mind raced. A position. A room. Safety.

"I—I don't know what to say," she stammered. "You barely know me."

"I know enough," Miss Chilton replied simply. "I've taught children for twelve years. I recognise when someone has the heart for it."

Annabelle felt a tangle of emotions rise within her—gratitude warring with suspicion, hope battling the hard-learned wariness of the orphanage. No one offered something for nothing. There was always a price, always disappointment waiting.

"This isn't charity," Miss Chilton added softly, as if reading her thoughts. "I need assistance, and you need a position. We would be helping each other."

Miss Chilton's offer hung between them. The orphanage had taught her caution—gifts came with conditions, kindness with expectations. Yet something in Miss Chilton's steady gaze spoke of genuine need rather than pity.

"I would be grateful for the opportunity," Annabelle said finally, her voice gaining strength with each word. "Teaching was my father's calling. Perhaps it might be mine as well."

Miss Chilton's face brightened. "Excellent! You can move your things tomorrow. It's not much—just a small room beneath the eaves—but it has a lovely view of the apple orchard."

A room of her own. After years of dormitory life at Thornfield, the very thought seemed luxurious beyond measure. No more bells dictating every moment, no more scrubbing floors until her knees bled, no more watching for Mr Pullter's scowl.

"Thank you," Annabelle whispered, emotion thickening her voice. "I'll work hard, I promise."

"I've no doubt of that," Miss Chilton replied, gathering her shawl. "Come, let's walk back to the doctor's. You'll need your rest before tomorrow."

As they stepped outside, the afternoon sun bathed Meadowbrook in golden light. Children played on the village green, their laughter carrying on the breeze. Mr Hadley nodded respectfully to Miss Chilton as they passed his shop, the scent of fresh bread wafting through the open door.

Annabelle clutched her Bible tighter. This place—this opportunity—felt like an answer to prayers she'd been too afraid to voice. The memory of Timothy's encouraging smile flashed through her mind. She wished he could see her now, standing on the precipice of a new beginning.

They paused at the crossroads where their paths would diverge—Miss Chilton to her cottage, Annabelle to Dr Miller's surgery for one final night.

"Until tomorrow, then," Miss Chilton said with a warm smile.

"Until tomorrow," Annabelle echoed.

She watched Miss Chilton's retreating figure before turning toward Dr Miller's. The village stretched before her, bathed in sunlight. For the first time since fleeing Thornfield, Annabelle felt something unfamiliar bloom in her chest—not just relief or gratitude, but genuine hope.

34
A ROOM OF HER OWN

Annabelle followed Miss Chilton along the winding lane that led away from the village square. Small cottages with thatched roofs lined the path, each with a garden plot bursting with summer vegetables and flowers. The late afternoon sun cast long shadows across the dirt road as they walked in companionable silence.

"Here we are," Miss Chilton announced, stopping before a modest stone cottage with climbing roses framing the door. "It's not grand, but it's home."

Annabelle's heart quickened as Miss Chilton opened the door and ushered her inside. The main room was simply furnished but neat—a small table with four chairs, a writing desk beneath the window, and a comfortable-looking armchair beside the hearth. Books lined the shelves on every wall, more books than Annabelle had seen since leaving her father's vicarage.

"Your room is upstairs," Miss Chilton said, leading the way up a narrow staircase. "Mind your head on the beam there."

At the top of the stairs, Miss Chilton opened a door to

reveal a small room tucked beneath the eaves. Annabelle stepped inside and caught her breath. A narrow bed with a patchwork quilt stood against one wall, a small chest of drawers against another. Beside the window sat a writing desk with a chair pulled up to it. Simple muslin curtains framed a view of Miss Chilton's garden, where roses and lavender nodded in the evening breeze.

"It's not much," Miss Chilton said, misinterpreting Annabelle's silence. "But the mattress is stuffed with fresh straw, and the quilt is warm in winter."

"It's perfect," Annabelle whispered, running her fingers along the smooth wooden surface of the desk.

A room of her own. Not a crowded dormitory with thirty other girls. A space that belonged to her alone.

She placed her father's Bible on the desk, the worn leather cover catching the last rays of sunlight streaming through the window. The book looked right there, as if it had been waiting for this moment.

"I thought you might use the desk for lesson planning," Miss Chilton said. "And for your own reading, of course."

Annabelle nodded, unable to speak past the lump in her throat. She touched the soft linens on the bed, marvelling at their cleanliness after years of rough blankets that never quite lost their musty smell.

Annabelle sat on the edge of the bed, smoothing her hand over the patchwork quilt. Seven years of sleeping on a thin straw pallet in Thornfield's crowded dormitory made this modest room seem like a palace. The walls here didn't echo with sobs or matrons' harsh commands. Instead, there was only the gentle rustling of leaves outside her window and distant birdsong.

She crossed to the window and gazed out at the garden below. The roses reminded her of her mother's garden at the vicarage, though these were different varieties. For a moment, she could almost hear her mother's voice explaining how to prune them properly.

"I'll leave you to settle in," Miss Chilton said from the doorway. "Supper will be ready in an hour. Nothing fancy—just bread, cheese and vegetable soup—but there's plenty of it."

The mention of plentiful food made Annabelle's stomach tighten with anticipation. At Thornfield, there had never been enough.

"Thank you, Miss Chilton," Annabelle said, turning from the window. "For everything."

After Miss Chilton departed, Annabelle returned to her father's Bible on the desk. She opened it carefully, finding the pressed bluebell that Timothy had given her years ago. Its colour had faded to a pale lavender, but it still carried memories of their friendship and shared dreams of freedom.

She wondered where Timothy was now. Had he reached Liverpool safely? Was he looking at the same evening sky, perhaps from the deck of a ship?

Annabelle closed the Bible gently and placed it in the drawer of her desk. For the first time since her parents died, she had a room of her own and work that would engage her mind rather than breaking her body. As the sunset painted the little room in gold, Annabelle felt something she hadn't experienced in years—the quiet stirring of hope.

35
WELCOME

Annabelle stood beside Miss Chilton in the village square the following Sunday after church service, her hands clasped tightly before her to hide their trembling. After a week of preparation at the cottage, this would be her formal introduction to Meadowbrook.

"Mrs Marsden, might I present Miss Annabelle Smith?" Miss Chilton's voice carried across the churchyard with practiced confidence. "She was governess to my cousin's children in Hertfordshire until my poor cousin's circumstances changed rather suddenly."

Annabelle felt a flush creep up her neck. The story was entirely fabricated, yet Miss Chilton delivered it with such conviction that even Annabelle almost believed it.

"Miss Smith will be assisting me at the school," Miss Chilton continued, addressing the small gathering of curious villagers. "She has a remarkable way with children, particularly those struggling with their letters."

"A governess, you say?" Mrs. Marsden, a plump woman

with shrewd eyes, assessed Annabelle. "And what of references, Miss Chilton?"

Annabelle's heart hammered against her ribs, but Miss Chilton merely smiled.

"Sadly, my cousin's financial collapse left many debts unpaid, including Miss Smith's wages. She departed without formal references, though I can personally vouch for her character and abilities."

The explanation flowed so naturally that the villagers nodded in understanding. Annabelle marvelled at how easily Miss Chilton had constructed a past that explained both her education and her lack of documentation.

"You speak very properly, Miss Smith," observed Mr Fletcher, Tommy's father. "My boy hasn't stopped talking about how you helped him read."

"She's quite transformed him," his wife added. "He actually asked for a book yesterday!"

Annabelle smiled, genuine warmth breaking through her anxiety. "Tommy is a bright boy. He simply needed a different approach."

More villagers approached, each greeting her with curious but kind expressions. Mrs Hadley pressed a small loaf of bread into her hands, "For your first week in the village, dear."

"You'll find Meadowbrook quite pleasant," the butcher's wife assured her. "Not like those fashionable towns where they look down their noses at newcomers."

Annabelle nodded and smiled, offering careful responses that revealed nothing of Thornfield or her true past. Each kind word and welcoming gesture eased the tightness in her chest, though caution remained her constant companion.

36
A NEW JOY

Annabelle arrived at the schoolhouse before dawn, arranging slates and chalk while Miss Chilton prepared the day's lessons. The small building smelled of wood polish and chalk dust—scents that had quickly become familiar and comforting after the acrid odours of Thornfield.

"I've prepared the arithmetic exercises for the older children," Annabelle said, smoothing her modest grey dress. "And I thought perhaps we might use the fable of the tortoise and the hare for the younger ones' reading practice."

Miss Chilton smiled. "You've a natural instinct for teaching, Annabelle. I daresay you were born for this."

The words warmed her more than she could express. At Thornfield, her mind had been an inconvenience, something to be subdued beneath endless physical labour. Here, it was her greatest asset.

As children filed in, Annabelle greeted each by name. Little Mary with her perpetually untied boot laces. William who chewed his pencils to splinters. Tommy Fletcher, now proudly carrying a slim book of his own.

"Miss Smith! Miss Smith!" Six-year-old Peter tugged at her skirt. "I found a frog in the garden and named him Solomon!"

"Like King Solomon from the Bible?" Annabelle knelt beside him. "What a wise choice for such a distinguished frog."

Peter beamed. "Can you tell us the story about Solomon today?"

"Perhaps during our midday rest," she promised.

Throughout the morning, Annabelle moved between groups of children, guiding their learning with gentle persistence. When Sarah struggled with her letters, Annabelle sat beside her, placing a reassuring hand on her shoulder.

"Remember how we spoke of building words like houses? First the foundation—these letters here—then the walls..."

The girl's face brightened as understanding dawned. "I've done it, Miss Smith! I've built 'garden'!"

Such moments sent joy coursing through Annabelle's veins. Each small victory reminded her of Timothy's face the first time he'd read a full verse from her father's Bible.

At midday, the children gathered around her on the floor as she told them about Solomon's wisdom.

"And when the two women both claimed the baby as their own, what did Solomon suggest?" she asked, watching their rapt faces.

"Cutting the baby in half!" shouted Thomas with alarming enthusiasm.

"But the real mother said no," Mary added solemnly. "Because she loved her baby more than winning."

"Precisely," Annabelle nodded. "Sometimes true wisdom means looking beyond what seems fair to find what is right."

The children peppered her with questions, their curiosity boundless. Annabelle answered each one thoughtfully, weaving connections between ancient stories and their daily lives in Meadowbrook.

For the first time since her parents' deaths, Annabelle felt truly alive.

37
BORROWED TIME

Annabelle straightened the row of slates after the children had departed, her movements methodical and precise. Through the schoolroom window, she observed two strangers on horseback passing through the village square. Her hands stilled. Though they showed no interest in the school, Annabelle's heart quickened. She ducked slightly, positioning herself behind the blackboard until they disappeared from view.

These moments of panic had become familiar companions. Despite her growing comfort in Meadowbrook, she remained constantly alert to potential threats. Each unfamiliar face in the village market sparked a flutter of anxiety. Every official-looking document Miss Chilton received made her stomach tighten until she confirmed it bore no mention of Thornfield or fugitives.

"You've polished those slates to perfection," Miss Chilton remarked, entering from the adjoining room. "Another five minutes and you'll wear holes through them."

Annabelle managed a smile. "Just ensuring they're ready for tomorrow."

Miss Chilton's gaze followed Annabelle's toward the window. "Those men were only passing through. Cattle traders, by the look of them."

"Of course," Annabelle replied, too quickly. "I was merely... admiring their horses."

Later, walking back to the cottage, Mrs Fallington stopped them to inquire about how Miss Smith was finding teaching at the school.

"Miss Smith has a remarkable way with numbers," Miss Chilton said. "She taught at a fine household in Hertfordshire, you know."

"Indeed?" Mrs Fallington's eyebrow arched. "And which family was that, Miss Smith?"

"The Westons," Annabelle answered smoothly, recalling the name she and Miss Chilton had decided on. "A private position. The children were quite advanced for their ages."

"How fascinating. My cousin knows several Westons. Perhaps—"

"A distant branch, I'm certain," Miss Chilton interrupted. "They kept rather to themselves."

In her room that evening, Annabelle sat at her window, watching darkness settle over Meadowbrook. She traced the roads with her eyes—the northern path that Timothy had taken toward Liverpool, the western road leading back toward Thornfield.

Miss Chilton knocked softly before entering with a cup of tea. "You needn't start at every knock, Annabelle. This is your home now."

"Thank you," Annabelle murmured, accepting the cup. "Old habits, I suppose."

"The past has a way of clinging to us," Miss Chilton said

gently. "But remember—you're Miss Smith here. The schoolmistress's assistant who helps children read and count and understand their world a little better each day."

Annabelle nodded, though her vigilance remained undiminished. She would continue watching the roads, measuring her words, and guarding her secret. The orphanage had taught her that safety was never guaranteed—only borrowed for a time.

38
THE NEW LIFE

Annabelle welcomed the last straggling students into the schoolroom. Two months had passed since her arrival in Meadowbrook, and the rhythm of village life had begun to feel natural, almost like breathing. The classroom no longer seemed foreign to her—the wooden desks arranged in neat rows, the slate boards stacked by the window, and the comforting smell of chalk dust hanging in the air.

"Good morning, Peter," she said to a freckled boy who hurried through the door. "Your sum work yesterday showed real improvement."

The boy beamed at her praise before scurrying to his seat. Annabelle watched him go with quiet satisfaction. These small moments—a child's progress, a question answered well, the spark of understanding in young eyes—filled her days with purpose.

In the evenings, Annabelle retreated to her room at Miss Chilton's cottage. There, with the window cracked open to catch the summer breeze, she would read from her father's Bible, tracing his handwritten notes in the margins. Sometimes, she would pause on a particular passage, remembering his voice as he'd explained its meaning during their evening readings at the vicarage.

"You've designed a wonderful lesson plan," Miss Chilton remarked one evening as they sat by the hearth, reviewing their work for the following day. "The children respond remarkably well to your methods."

"I find they learn best when encouraged rather than frightened," Annabelle replied, thinking of the harsh discipline at Thornfield. "My father always said knowledge should be offered like bread, not forced like medicine."

Miss Chilton smiled warmly. "Your father sounds like a wise man. I would have enjoyed meeting him."

These conversations had become precious to Annabelle. Miss Chilton never pressed for details about Thornfield or questioned the gaps in Annabelle's stories. Instead, she offered friendship freely, sharing her own dreams of expanding the school someday and teaching Annabelle the practical aspects of running a classroom.

"I've been thinking," Miss Chilton said, pouring them both more tea, "we might introduce some natural science lessons. The children could collect specimens from the meadow—pressed flowers, interesting stones."

"That would be wonderful," Annabelle agreed, already imagining the children's excitement. "We could create a display table by the window."

Together, they sketched out plans for new lessons, debated teaching approaches, and occasionally shared quiet laughter over the day's small mishaps. In these moments, Annabelle felt the orphanage receding further into the past, though never completely vanishing from her thoughts.

39
EXCITING RUMOURS

Annabelle felt the ripple of excitement through the village before she heard the news properly. It started with whispers between the mothers as they collected their children from school, heads bent together in animated conversation. Then came the unusual bustle in the village square as she and Miss Chilton walked home, with people gathering in small clusters despite the afternoon heat.

"What's happening?" Annabelle asked as Mrs Finchly, energeticly passed them.

"Haven't you heard? We're getting a new vicar!" The woman's eyes sparkled with the delight of sharing fresh gossip. "Reverend Edward Woolworth, all the way from London. Young too—barely six-and-twenty, they say."

Annabelle's heart gave a peculiar lurch at the word "vicar." For a moment, she was back in St Michael's parish, watching her father in his study.

"When does he arrive?" Miss Chilton inquired, her practical nature cutting through the excitement.

"Next Tuesday. The bishop himself recommended him."

Mrs Finchly leaned closer. "They say he has most progressive ideas about education. Worked in the poorest parishes in London, teaching children to read and write who'd never have had the chance otherwise."

This caught Annabelle's attention. She thought of Timothy and the other children at Thornfield, denied the simplest opportunities for learning.

By the following morning, the village buzzed like a disturbed beehive. Annabelle overheard fragments of conversation as she arranged slates for the day's lessons.

"...studied at Oxford, I heard..."

"...quite handsome, according to Mrs Pembroke's niece who saw him at the bishop's residence..."

"...not at all like old Reverend Grimes with his fire and brimstone..."

The children arrived full of the news too, barely able to focus on their letters.

"Miss Smith," little Sarah tugged at her skirt during the morning lesson, "is it true the new vicar wants to start a library for children?"

"I couldn't say," Annabelle replied gently. "We shall have to wait and see what Reverend Woolworth brings to Meadowbrook."

But privately, Annabelle felt a flutter of curiosity. A vicar who valued education might be a powerful ally for the school. Yet the thought of regular interaction with a man of the cloth—someone who might remind her of her father—stirred complicated feelings she had carefully tucked away.

40
AN ALLY

Annabelle stood with Miss Chilton and the other villagers gathered in front of St Matthew's Church, watching the approaching carriage. The entire village had turned out to welcome the new vicar, with even the shopkeepers closing early for the occasion. Mrs Fallington had positioned herself and her daughter, Clara, at the front of the crowd, both wearing their finest dresses despite the warm afternoon.

"There he is," someone whispered as the carriage door swung open.

Annabelle found herself rising on tiptoes for a better view, curiosity getting the better of her usual caution around church matters. Reverend Edward Woolworth stepped down from the carriage with surprising agility, looking much younger than Annabelle had expected. At twenty-six, he possessed a vitality that immediately distinguished him from old Reverend Grimes, whose sermons had often sent half the congregation to sleep.

The new vicar smiled broadly as he greeted the welcoming

committee. His clerical attire looked slightly rumpled from the journey, but his bright blue eyes sparkled with genuine warmth as he shook hands with the church wardens.

"Welcome to Meadowbrook, Reverend Woolworth," Mr Hadley said, pumping the young man's hand enthusiastically.

"Thank you for such a kind reception," Reverend Woolworth replied, his voice carrying clearly across the churchyard. "I look forward to serving this community and getting to know each of you."

Annabelle noticed how he took time with each person, asking questions and listening intently to their responses rather than merely nodding politely. When Mrs. Fletcher mentioned her son Tommy's struggles with reading, the vicar's face lit up with interest.

"I believe education is vital for every child, regardless of their circumstances," he said earnestly. "In my previous parish in London, we established reading circles for children who couldn't attend proper schools. I'd be delighted to discuss how we might support your son's learning."

Several parents exchanged hopeful glances at this. Reverend Grimes had shown little interest in education, considering it primarily the domain of those who could afford it.

"You see," Miss Chilton whispered to Annabelle, "perhaps we shall have an ally after all."

41
FREQUENT VISITOR

Annabelle arranged the slates on each desk with methodical care, enjoying the quiet of the schoolroom before the children arrived. She looked up at the sound of footsteps and saw Reverend Woolworth entering alongside Miss Chilton, his tall figure ducking slightly beneath the low doorframe.

"Good morning, Miss Smith," he called cheerfully, using the name she had adopted in Meadowbrook. "Miss Chilton has kindly allowed me to observe your lessons today."

"Of course, Reverend," Annabelle replied, feeling a flutter of nervousness. This marked his third visit to the school in as many weeks.

The children filed in shortly after, their usual morning chatter falling to whispers when they spotted the vicar. Tommy Fletcher broke the tension by rushing forward.

"Reverend Woolworth! I finished that book you lent me!"

The vicar's face brightened. "Did you indeed? And what did you think of Robinson Crusoe's adventures?"

As Tommy launched into an enthusiastic retelling,

Annabelle noticed how Reverend Woolworth knelt to the boy's level, giving him his complete attention. It reminded her painfully of her father's manner with his parishioners' children.

Throughout the morning, Annabelle found herself increasingly aware of the vicar's presence as he moved about the classroom. He didn't merely observe but participated, helping little Sarah form her letters and encouraging James with his sums. The children responded to him with an ease that surprised her, their usual shyness melting away under his gentle questions and genuine interest.

During the midday break, Annabelle overheard him speaking with Miss Chilton by the window.

"What you've accomplished here is remarkable," he said. "But imagine what more we could do with a proper library. Even a small collection would make such a difference."

"The cost would be prohibitive," Miss Chilton sighed. "Most families here can barely afford the school fees."

"Perhaps we might arrange something with the parish funds," he suggested. "A partnership between church and school. After all, education and spiritual growth go hand in hand, wouldn't you agree?"

Annabelle found herself nodding silently as she arranged papers at her desk, struck by the vicar's progressive thinking. In her experience, clergymen rarely concerned themselves with matters of education beyond Sunday school.

His enthusiasm seemed to fill the small schoolroom, breathing new life into their daily routines. For the first time since arriving in Meadowbrook, Annabelle felt a sense of possibility expanding before her—not just for herself, but for the children she'd grown to care for deeply.

∼

Annabelle observed the way Reverend Woolworth leaned forward in his chair, his attention fully captured by Miss Chilton's animated description of yesterday's lessons. The three of them sat in the empty schoolroom after the children had departed, afternoon sunlight streaming through the windows and catching dust motes that danced between them.

"Young Sarah has made remarkable progress with her letters," Miss Chilton explained. "Miss Smith devised a method of teaching that connects each letter to a story. The children adore it."

The Reverend's gaze shifted to Annabelle, curiosity brightening his eyes. "Is that so? Where did you learn such techniques, Miss Smith?"

Annabelle's fingers tightened around her teacup. "My father believed learning should bring joy, not dread," she answered carefully. "I merely adapted his philosophy."

"Your father sounds like a wise man," Edward replied. "Was he a teacher as well?"

A flash of panic coursed through her. "He valued education greatly," she said, sidestepping the direct question.

"Miss Smith has a natural gift," Miss Chilton interjected, sensing Annabelle's discomfort. "You should see how the children flock to her during reading hour."

Edward nodded, his expression thoughtful. "I've been considering ways we might expand educational opportunities here in Meadowbrook. Perhaps a lending library to start, with evening reading circles for parents who wish to improve their own literacy."

"The adults would benefit tremendously," Annabelle found herself saying. "Many cannot read the Bible themselves and rely solely on what they hear in church."

"Precisely my thinking," Edward agreed, his face lighting

up. "Would you consider helping me organise such an endeavour, Miss Smith? Your experience would be invaluable."

The warmth of his enthusiasm melted something long-frozen within her. "I would be honoured, Reverend."

Over the following weeks, Edward became a frequent visitor to the schoolhouse. Their discussions extended beyond the day's lessons to ambitious plans for Meadowbrook's future. Annabelle found herself contributing ideas born from her own childhood at the vicarage and the stark contrast of Thornfield, where knowledge was treated as dangerous rather than liberating.

"What if we created a system where older children could tutor younger ones?" she suggested one afternoon as they walked back to Miss Chilton's cottage. "It would reinforce their own learning while helping those who struggle."

Edward's approving nod sent an unexpected flutter through her chest. "Brilliant. We could implement that immediately."

Yet even as Annabelle found herself drawn into these hopeful collaborations, a shadow lurked at the edges of her consciousness. Each time a stranger passed through the village, she felt her muscles tense. Every official-looking document that crossed Miss Chilton's desk made her heart skip a beat. The fear that someone from Thornfield might recognise her—or worse, that notices about her escape might reach Meadowbrook—never fully subsided.

42
NECESSARY DECEPTION

Annabelle noticed how Edward's visits to the schoolroom grew more frequent as summer dissolved into autumn. He would arrive with books tucked under his arm, his clerical collar slightly askew, as if he'd hurried across the village green.

"Miss Smith," he called one afternoon as the children filed out for their midday meal, "I've been pondering something in Ecclesiastes that I'd welcome your thoughts on."

Annabelle glanced up from the slate she was wiping clean. "Which passage, Reverend?"

"The one concerning wisdom and folly. Do you believe wisdom brings greater happiness, or merely greater awareness of life's sorrows?"

The question stirred memories of her father's study, where similar discussions had filled evening hours. Without thinking, Annabelle quoted, "'For with much wisdom comes much sorrow; the more knowledge, the more grief.' Yet I've always found comfort in understanding, even when the understanding brings pain."

Edward's eyebrows rose slightly. "That's precisely the tension I've been contemplating. Most governesses I've encountered focus solely on rote learning rather than interpretation."

Heat crept into Annabelle's cheeks. She'd spoken too freely, revealing knowledge beyond what would be expected of her supposed background.

"My father encouraged questioning," she said carefully. "He believed faith should be examined, not merely accepted."

Their theological discussions became a quiet ritual. Edward would appear after lessons, sometimes bringing passages that had troubled him during sermon preparation. Annabelle found herself drawn to his genuine curiosity, so different from Reverend Bloom's performance based piety.

"You speak of scripture as if it's alive," Edward remarked one day as they walked through the schoolyard.

"Isn't that how we should approach it?" Annabelle replied. "Not as dead words but as living guidance?"

His smile then—warm and appreciative—sent an unfamiliar flutter through her chest. It was a feeling both wonderful and terrifying. For every moment of connection, a shadow of fear followed. What would he think if he knew the truth? That she was not Miss Smith the governess but Annabelle Sinclair, fugitive?

They exchanged books—Edward lending her theological commentaries, Annabelle sharing teaching approaches. Their hands would brush during these exchanges, and sometimes Edward's lingered a moment longer than necessary. Each time, Annabelle felt torn between pulling away and wishing for more.

"I've never met anyone who understands faith quite as you do," Edward told her one afternoon as they shelved books in the small library they'd established. "It's refreshing to speak without pretence."

Annabelle turned away, busying herself with straightening a row of primers. The irony cut deep—their connection was built on understanding, yet founded upon her necessary deception.

43
PEOPLE WATCHING

Annabelle noticed the whispers first. They rippled through the churchyard after Sunday service—conversations that ceased when she approached, only to resume with greater intensity once she passed. The way Mrs Hadley's smile tightened when Edward paused to discuss a passage with her. The sudden coolness from women who had welcomed her warmly mere weeks before.

"Did you see them after service?" Annabelle overheard Mrs Finchly murmur to another woman as they collected their prayer books. "Heads bent together like conspirators. Hardly proper for a man of the cloth."

"And with a woman of such mysterious origins," came the reply. "No family to speak of, no proper references. Makes one wonder."

Annabelle's cheeks burned as she pretended absorption in straightening the children's slates. Their friendship had become the village's favourite subject of speculation, transforming something pure into something tainted by suspicion.

The situation worsened when Mrs Fallington swept into the schoolroom one afternoon, ostensibly to discuss her charitable contribution to the library fund. Her daughter Clara trailed behind, a pretty girl with carefully arranged golden curls.

"Miss Smith," Mrs Fallington's voice carried the precise chill of winter frost, "I wonder if you might explain the nature of your... consultations with Reverend Woolworth. The parish council has expressed concern about his frequent visits here."

"We discuss educational matters for the children," Annabelle replied, keeping her voice steady despite her racing heart. "The Reverend has been most supportive of our teaching methods."

"Indeed." Mrs Fallington's gaze swept the modest schoolroom. "One wonders what educational insights a young woman of your limited experience might offer a Cambridge-educated clergyman. Perhaps your time would be better spent focusing on the younger children's basic needs rather than engaging our vicar in matters beyond your station."

That evening, Miss Chilton gently broached the subject over supper.

"You should know Mrs Fallington has been quite vocal at the Ladies' Aid Society," she said, passing Annabelle the bread. "She's suggesting the Reverend's attention to our school—to you in particular—distracts from his wider parish duties."

"She wishes her daughter to catch his eye," Annabelle said quietly.

"Indeed. The Fallington estate would make a handsome addition to any clergyman's prospects." Miss Chilton sighed. "I fear your friendship has become a target for those who cannot understand it—or who have reasons to undermine it."

Annabelle set down her spoon, appetite gone. The fragile peace she'd built in Meadowbrook suddenly felt precarious.

Each interaction with Edward now carried the weight of public scrutiny, transforming their innocent exchanges into potential scandal.

"People are watching," Miss Chilton added gently. "And not all with kind intentions."

44
GUARDIAN STARS

Annabelle's fingers trembled as she arranged hymnals before the parish meeting. The church hall buzzed with voices, Mrs Fallington's carrying above the rest as she held court among a circle of nodding parishioners. Annabelle kept her head down, focusing on her task rather than the sideways glances cast her way.

Edward entered, his smile warming when he spotted her. He crossed the room to help with the final preparations, their hands briefly touching as they arranged the last books.

"Our library project progresses well," he said. "The children's enthusiasm for reading—"

Mrs Fallington's voice cut through their conversation like a knife. "Reverend Woolworth, might I suggest you attend to the matter of the leaking church roof before indulging in frivolous reading circles? The parish council has expressed concern about your... priorities."

The room fell silent. Every eye turned toward them.

"The education of our children is hardly frivolous, Mrs Fallington," Edward replied evenly.

"Perhaps not, but your constant attentions to Miss Smith certainly appear so." Her lips curved into a thin smile. "A vicar should maintain certain standards of propriety, especially with a woman of such... uncertain background."

Murmurs of agreement rippled through the gathering. Annabelle's cheeks burned as she stared at the floor, wishing it might open and swallow her whole.

Edward straightened, his voice firm but controlled. "Miss Smith has demonstrated exceptional dedication to our children's education. Her character and capabilities speak for themselves through her work. I would expect Christian charity rather than unfounded suspicion from this parish."

The defence, though gentle, silenced the whispers. Mrs Fallington's face hardened as Edward continued discussing parish business as if the confrontation had never occurred.

Later, walking back to Miss Chilton's cottage alone, Annabelle wrapped her shawl tightly around her shoulders against the evening chill. Edward's defence had touched her deeply, yet filled her with dread. His reputation now suffered because of her secrets.

How could she maintain this deception? Each day brought fresh risk of exposure. If the truth emerged about Thornfield and her escape, Edward would face humiliation for defending a fugitive.

That night, Annabelle sat at her small desk, Father's Bible open before her. The pressed bluebell from Timothy marked the passage about truth setting one free. Yet truth threatened everything she'd built here.

Annabelle closed her bedroom window against the evening chill, but lingered by the glass. Stars punctured the inky canvas above Meadowbrook, reminding her of nights at Thornfield when she and Timothy would count them through gaps in the dormitory roof. Tonight, however, her thoughts weren't with

Timothy but with Edward—the way he'd defended her before Mrs Fallington and the entire parish.

She pressed her forehead against the cool glass. What foolishness to allow her heart such dangerous freedom. A vicar and a fugitive from the orphanage? The very notion was absurd.

"He sees a teacher, a colleague in faith—nothing more," she whispered to herself, breath fogging the window. "And that must be enough."

Annabelle moved to her small desk where her father's Bible lay open. Her fingers traced the familiar marginalia, his neat script offering commentary on passages that had sustained her through the darkest nights at Thornfield.

The stars outside cast just enough light for her to make out the words: "To everything there is a season, and a time to every purpose under heaven."

What was this season in her life? One of hiding and fear, certainly. But also one of purpose—of teaching children who reminded her daily of herself and Timothy, of conversations that nourished her mind and spirit after years of starvation.

And Edward—his presence illuminated corners of her heart long left dark. His passion for education, his genuine faith, his kindness that expected nothing in return. These were gifts she'd never anticipated finding in Meadowbrook.

"I cannot lose this," she murmured, closing the Bible gently. Whatever grew between them—this friendship, this understanding—it must be protected, even if it could never become what her treacherous heart sometimes whispered it might.

Annabelle moved back to the window. The stars remained steadfast above, unchanging despite the turmoil below. She would be like them—constant, true to her purpose here, guarding her secret while holding fast to the connection that gave her life new meaning.

45
PANIC

A year had passed since Annabelle had arrived in Meadowbrook. The crisp autumn days had given way to winter's bite before yielding to spring's gentle touch, matching the growing sense of belonging that had taken root in Annabelle's heart. Each morning, she woke in her small room at Miss Chilton's cottage, still marvelling at the luxury of privacy after years in Thornfield's crowded dormitory.

Sometimes, when she caught her reflection in the window glass, she hardly recognised herself. The hollow-cheeked girl had vanished, replaced by a young woman with colour in her cheeks and purpose in her step.

Yet beneath this newfound contentment lurked the shadow of her past. Each unfamiliar face that passed through the village square sent a flutter of anxiety through her chest. Each official-looking document posted on the church door made her heart skip.

On market day, Annabelle noticed a change in the village atmosphere. The usual cheerful bartering had been replaced by hushed conversations and troubled glances. Villagers huddled in small groups, their faces drawn with concern.

"What's happening?" she asked Mrs Fletcher as she selected apples from her stall.

"Haven't you seen, Miss Smith? The notices by the town hall."

Annabelle's hand froze mid-reach. "Notices?"

Following Mrs Fletcher's gesture, she moved toward the bulletin board where several villagers had gathered. Excusing herself, she edged through the small crowd until she could see the paper nailed to the wooden surface.

The world tilted beneath her feet.

INFORMATION SOUGHT: Young woman, approximately seventeen years of age, with distinctive red hair, escaped from Thornfield Orphanage. Accused of violently assaulting a carriage driver. Reward offered for information leading to her capture.

Annabelle's stomach clenched. Her throat closed. The description—her description—seemed to leap from the page, the words burning into her vision.

Assault? She had done nothing but flee with Timothy. Had the driver claimed violence to save his own position? Or was this fabrication meant to ensure her return, painting her as dangerous rather than desperate?

Why were they searching for her now? It had been a year! Annabelle couldn't shake the feeling that the search for her had a deeper agenda than simply reclaiming a lost worker.

She forced herself to breathe normally, to keep her expression neutral as panic coursed through her veins. Everything she had built here—her position, her friendships, the respect she had earned—all balanced on the edge of a knife.

At least they weren't also searching for Timothy. At least he was, hopefully, completely free.

46
THE BISHOP

Edward Woolworth strode back to the vicarage with the letter clutched in his hand, pulse quickening with each step. The Bishop's seal—unmistakable, formal, and somehow intimidating—had caught him off guard when he'd broken it open at the post office.

"Bishop Harrington," he muttered, pushing open the heavy oak door. "Coming here. To Meadowbrook."

The sitting room felt suddenly inadequate, its modest furnishings poor reflections of his ambitions. Edward paced the worn carpet, rereading the crisp penmanship that announced Bishop Darius Harrington would grace St Matthew's in a fortnight's time.

A knock at the door interrupted his thoughts.

"Reverend?" Mrs Hadley peered in, basket of fresh bread in hand. "I've brought your usual, and—" She stopped, noticing his distracted expression. "Is everything all right?"

"Bishop Harrington is coming to evaluate the parish." The words tumbled out before he could arrange them properly.

Mrs Hadley's eyes widened. "The Bishop himself? Goodness me."

"Indeed." Edward smoothed the letter against the table. "This could be my opportunity, Mrs Hadley. The educational reforms I've been advocating—the Bishop has influence throughout the diocese. If he approves of our work here..."

"Then your ideas might spread beyond our little village." Mrs Hadley nodded knowingly. "The reading circles and the library..."

"Precisely." Edward felt a surge of excitement cutting through his apprehension. "Children in parishes across the county might benefit. Not just those fortunate enough to have parents who value education."

By noon, word had spread through Meadowbrook like wildfire. Edward found himself cornered in the village square by half a dozen eager parishioners.

"Is it true, Reverend?" Mr Fletcher asked. "Bishop Harrington himself?"

"The man who convinced Parliament to fund three new church schools?" Mrs Finchly added.

Edward nodded. "The very same."

"My cousin in Canterbury says his sermons draw crowds from three parishes over," whispered Mrs Bennett. "And the Duke of Northumberland consults him on charitable matters."

"They say he's the youngest bishop in a century to publish theological works," added Mr Marsden. "Brilliant mind, by all accounts."

Edward felt the weight of their expectations pressing upon him. "I hope to show him that even our small parish can be forward-thinking in its approach."

"You'll impress him, Reverend," Mrs Fletcher said firmly. "Tommy's reading has come along wonderfully since you started those evening classes."

Edward smiled, though his mind raced with preparations. The Bishop's approval could open doors he'd only dreamed of—opportunities to implement the educational reforms he'd advocated since his days in London's poorest parishes.

"We must ensure everything is perfect," he said, straightening his shoulders. "This visit could change everything."

47
REALISATION

Annabelle lingered near the village bakery, pretending to examine Mrs Hadley's fresh loaves while straining to hear the conversation between two women at the counter. Their excited voices carried through the warm, yeasty air.

"Bishop Harrington's sermons changed my cousin's life entirely. She wrote that his teachings on Christian charity are without equal."

"And to think he'll be here in Meadowbrook! What an honour for Reverend Woolworth."

Annabelle's fingers tightened around her basket handle. Bishop Harrington. The name tugged at something in her memory, though she couldn't place why it unsettled her so.

Later that afternoon, Edward arrived at the schoolroom as Annabelle was arranging books for the following day's lessons.

"I've brought something for you," he said, his eyes bright with enthusiasm. He placed a leather-bound volume on her desk. "Bishop Harrington's treatise on divine providence. It made his reputation throughout the Church of England. I thought you might enjoy reading it before his visit."

"Thank you," Annabelle murmured, running her fingers over the gilt lettering.

That evening, seated by her bedroom window, Annabelle opened the book. Her eyes widened as she read the first chapter. The phrasing, the examples, the particular way certain biblical passages were interpreted—they were hauntingly familiar.

She turned page after page, her heart beating faster. A passage about the Book of Job struck her with particular force. Her father had explained it in precisely the same unusual way, drawing parallels to the Israelites' wandering that few theologians made.

Memories surfaced of sitting in her father's study at ten years old, watching him write feverishly in his notebooks. "God reveals Himself in our suffering," he'd told her, "not despite it but through it." The exact words stared back at her from the Bishop's treatise.

The book slipped from Annabelle's trembling fingers. Cold dread seeped through her body. These weren't merely similar ideas—these were her father's thoughts, his unique interpretations, sometimes, his very words.

She recalled Reverend Bloom sorting through her father's papers after his death, pocketing certain manuscripts before sending her to Thornfield. The connection crystallised with terrible clarity.

The dread of the Bishop's visit now had a shape—not just the fear of being recognised as a fugitive from Thornfield, but something deeper. Something connected to her father's legacy, stolen and claimed by another.

The familiar terror of discovery crashed over her. She imagined being dragged back to Thornfield, or worse, to Thatchwood Mill. The orphanage's grey walls and hollow-eyed children flashed through her mind. The sound of Mr Pullter's heavy footsteps. The endless, grinding labour that broke both body and spirit.

Meadowbrook, with its schoolroom and cottage and children who looked at her with trust instead of resignation, seemed suddenly as fragile as a soap bubble, ready to burst at the slightest touch.

Annabelle clutched the Bishop's book to her chest as she made her way downstairs. Her heart hammered against her ribs like a trapped bird. The cottage was quiet save for the gentle clinking of teacups from the kitchen. Miss Chilton would be having her evening tea—the perfect moment to speak with her.

She found Miss Chilton seated at the small wooden table, a pot of chamomile steaming before her.

"Annabelle, dear. Would you care to join me?" Miss Chilton's smile faltered as she caught sight of Annabelle's face. "Whatever is the matter?"

Annabelle sank into the chair opposite. "I saw the notices in the village today."

Miss Chilton's hand paused midway to her cup. "Notices?"

"By the town hall. They're searching for a red-haired young woman who supposedly attacked a carriage driver." Annabelle's voice dropped to a whisper. "They're looking for me."

Miss Chilton reached across the table and clasped Annabelle's trembling hands. "After all this time? Why now?"

"I don't know." Annabelle swallowed the lump in her throat. She considered mentioning the Bishop, the stolen words, the terrible coincidence—but stopped herself. It would only complicate matters, and Miss Chilton had already risked enough by sheltering her. "Perhaps someone recognised me. Perhaps Mr Pullter never stopped looking."

"Listen to me," Miss Chilton said firmly. "You've built a life here—a good life. The children adore you. The parents respect you. You belong in Meadowbrook now."

"But if someone discovers—"

"Then we shall face it together." Miss Chilton's grip tightened. "I didn't bring you into my home, into my school, only to abandon you at the first sign of trouble."

Tears pricked at Annabelle's eyes. "I've put you at risk."

"Nonsense. I made my choice when I saw you teaching Tommy Fletcher." Miss Chilton poured a second cup of tea and pushed it towards Annabelle. "Now, we must be practical. Continue as normal—teach your lessons, help with the library preparations. Draw no undue attention to yourself."

"And if someone comes asking questions?"

"Then I shall answer them." Miss Chilton's eyes flashed with determination. "You focus on your work. Your students need you, Annabelle."

Annabelle nodded, wrapping her fingers around the warm teacup. The knot of fear in her stomach loosened slightly. Whatever came, she would not face it alone.

48
A CLOSE CALL

Annabelle arranged the hymn books in the vestry, her fingers working methodically as her mind raced with thoughts of the Bishop's impending visit. The church had filled quickly this morning, parishioners eager to catch a glimpse of the distinguished visitor. Through the screen separating the vestry from the nave, she observed the congregation settling into their pews, their Sunday best gleaming in the light filtering through the stained glass windows.

The heavy oak door creaked open, letting in a gust of damp air. Mr Silas Penrose entered, shaking raindrops from his worn woollen coat. Annabelle froze. The sight of him—stooped with age but still possessing the same kind eyes and weathered face—transported her instantly back to St Michael's parish. How many times had he patted her head after her father's sermons, slipping her peppermint sweets when no one was looking?

She shrank back behind a pillar, praying he wouldn't notice her. But fate had other plans. As he settled into a pew near the front, his gaze wandered toward the vestry and caught on her figure. His rheumy eyes widened, recognition dawning across his face like sunrise.

"Bless my soul," he exclaimed, rising to his feet with surprising agility. "Annabelle Sinclair! Reverend Thomas's little girl!"

His voice, though cracked with age, carried through the hushed church with terrible clarity. The hymn book slipped from Annabelle's numb fingers, landing with a thud that seemed to echo her thundering heartbeat.

Several heads turned. Mrs Fallington's daughter Clara, who had been adjusting her bonnet, whipped around, her mouth falling open in shock. The whispers began immediately, rippling through the congregation like wind through wheat.

"Sinclair? Did he say Sinclair?"

"I thought her name was Smith..."

"A Vicar's daughter?"

Cold fear pooled in Annabelle's stomach. The carefully constructed facade of Miss Smith—the respectable governess from Hertfordshire—crumbled around her. Every cautious step she'd taken, every half-truth she'd told, every detail she'd omitted—all undone by a moment of innocent recognition.

Her gaze met Clara Fallington's triumphant stare across the church. The young woman's lips curved into a satisfied smile as she leaned toward her mother, whispering urgently.

Annabelle's breath caught in her throat as dozens of curious faces turned toward her. Mrs Fallington's narrowed eyes gleamed with suspicion, and even Miss Chilton appeared startled, her brow furrowing with concern.

The whispers grew louder. Someone mentioned the notices about a red-haired fugitive. Annabelle's instincts screamed at her to flee. With practiced quietness honed through years at Thornfield, she edged backward, keeping to the shadows of the vestry. Her fingers found the latch of the side door—the one that led to the cemetery rather than through the nave.

The cool air struck her face as she slipped outside, her skirt brushing against the weathered gravestones. The rain had softened to a gentle mist that clung to her hair and eyelashes. Annabelle's heart hammered against her ribs as she hurried along the path that wound behind the church.

Anger surged through her veins—anger at Reverend Bloom for stealing her father's writings, anger at the unfairness of a world that had forced her to hide who she truly was, anger at herself for daring to believe she could outrun her past. Yet beneath the anger lay a profound longing for the security of her childhood at the vicarage, where her identity had been a source of pride rather than danger.

The rain-slicked path stretched before her, as uncertain as her future. Each step took her further from the sanctuary she'd found in Meadowbrook, from the children who trusted her, from Edward whose company had begun to mean more than she dared admit. There was no safe haven now—not when her true name had been spoken aloud within these village walls.

A day passed with no sign of Silas Penrose, but Annabelle felt the change in the village like a physical weight. Shopkeepers who had once greeted her warmly, now studied her with guarded expressions. Children's parents collected them promptly after lessons, cutting short the conversations that had once flowed easily. Even Miss Chilton's reassurances couldn't dispel the cloud of suspicion that hung over Annabelle like the persistent drizzle outside.

49
AN OLD FACE

Annabelle felt the weight of suspicious stares as she crossed the village square. The market bustled with its usual activity, but conversations died whenever she approached, only to resume in hushed whispers once she passed. Mrs Hadley, who had once pressed fresh bread into her hands with motherly affection, now averted her eyes, busying herself with arranging her wares. The butcher's wife whispered something to the milliner, both glancing in Annabelle's direction before quickly looking away.

Each step felt heavier than the last. Annabelle clutched her basket tighter, her knuckles whitening. She had known this moment might come—had feared it since arriving in Meadowbrook—yet the reality cut deeper than she'd imagined. The careful life she'd constructed was unravelling thread by thread.

"Did you hear? Calling herself Smith when she's really a Sinclair... allegedly of course..."

"...ran away from somewhere..."

"...those notices about a red-haired girl..."

The fragments of conversation sliced through her like knives. Annabelle kept her gaze fixed on the cobblestones, refusing to let the villagers see how their words wounded her. She'd survived Thornfield's cruelties; she would endure this too.

"Miss Smith."

Edward's voice, clear and steady, cut through the murmurs. Annabelle looked up to find him standing before her, his blue eyes meeting hers without hesitation or judgment. Unlike the others, his gaze held no suspicion—only concern and something warmer that made her heart flutter despite everything.

"Reverend Woolworth," she acknowledged, aware of the many eyes watching their exchange.

"May I walk with you?" he asked, offering his arm.

She hesitated, thinking of the gossip this would fuel. "I wouldn't wish to compromise your position further."

"Let me worry about that," Edward said, his voice low but firm. He stepped closer, speaking for her ears alone. "I won't have you face this alone, Annabelle. Whatever your past holds, whatever name you've carried—it changes nothing of the person I've come to know."

"You don't understand what's at stake," she whispered.

"Then help me understand." His eyes held steady on hers. "I'm not abandoning you to face these whispers alone. We'll navigate this together."

Annabelle stared at Edward, his steadfast loyalty warming something deep within her that had grown cold with fear. Before she could respond, her attention caught on a figure moving through the market crowd. Something about the confident stride, the set of the shoulders...

She blinked, certain her mind was playing tricks. It couldn't be.

But it was.

Timothy.

Her Timothy, no longer the wiry boy from Thornfield but a man with broad shoulders and sun-bronzed skin. He moved with purpose, scanning the faces around him until his eyes locked with hers.

"Timothy?" His name escaped her lips as a question, though her heart already knew the answer.

The basket slipped from her fingers, forgotten. Annabelle's feet carried her forward without conscious thought, weaving through startled villagers. She crashed into him with such force that he staggered backwards, but his arms encircled her immediately, solid and real.

"Belle," he whispered, using the name only he had ever called her. "I found you."

Annabelle clung to him, burying her face against his shoulder. He smelled of salt and distant places, but underneath was the familiar scent that was uniquely Timothy. Tears spilled down her cheeks as she pulled back to look at him properly.

"How?" was all she could manage.

"I've been searching for months," Timothy said, his voice deeper than she remembered but with the same warmth. "Liverpool first, like I planned, got work on the docks loading cargo. But I couldn't settle, not without knowing you were safe."

His hands gripped her shoulders, eyes drinking in the sight of her as though afraid she might vanish.

"I went east like you said, asking after a red-haired teacher in every village. When I heard about Meadowbrook's new schoolmistress assistant with copper curls..." His voice broke. "I knew it had to be you."

"You've been looking all this time?" Annabelle whispered,

overwhelmed by the thought of him searching for her while she built her new life.

"Did you think I wouldn't?" Timothy's smile was the same one that had sustained her through Thornfield's darkest days. "We promised, Belle. Remember?"

50
REUNION

Annabelle stood frozen between the two men who represented such different parts of her life—Timothy, her anchor through the darkest years at Thornfield, and Edward, who embodied the promise of her new beginning in Meadowbrook. The market square had fallen eerily quiet, villagers watching the scene unfold with undisguised curiosity.

Edward approached them, his expression unreadable. Annabelle's heart hammered against her ribs. What must he think of this strange reunion?

"Perhaps we might continue this conversation somewhere more private," Edward suggested, his voice low but kind. "My parish house is just beyond the churchyard."

Relief washed over Annabelle. "Yes, thank you." She turned to Timothy, who was eyeing Edward with cautious appraisal. "Timothy, this is Reverend Edward Woolworth. Reverend, this is Timothy... my dearest friend from—" she stopped herself.

"A pleasure to meet you, Timothy," Edward extended his

hand without hesitation. "Any friend of Miss Smith's is welcome here in Meadowbrook."

Timothy's eyebrows rose slightly at the unfamiliar name attributed to Annabelle, but he clasped the offered hand firmly. "Likewise, Reverend."

They walked in silence through the village, Annabelle acutely aware of curtains twitching and faces peering from shop windows as they passed. The modest parish house stood in the shadow of St Matthew's Church, its small garden neat but simple.

Inside, Edward's sitting room felt warm and lived-in, with books stacked on nearly every surface. He stoked the fire while Annabelle and Timothy settled into worn armchairs.

"I still can't believe I found you," Timothy said, leaning forward with his elbows on his knees. "Liverpool was brutal at first—sleeping in doorways, fighting for work each morning at the docks. But I kept thinking of you, wondering if you'd found somewhere safe."

Annabelle's throat tightened. "I thought of you every day."

"I kept asking after a red-haired teacher," Timothy continued, excitement building in his voice. "Most people thought I was daft, but I knew you'd find a way to teach. Just like you taught me with Reverend Sinclair's Bible."

Edward's head lifted sharply.

"Your father would be proud, Belle," Timothy pressed on, oblivious to his slip. "The way he loved teaching you about scripture—I remember all those stories you told me about him. Reverend Thomas Sinclair's daughter, continuing his work in her own way."

Annabelle's eyes darted to Edward, whose expression had shifted from polite interest to dawning realisation.

Annabelle felt her carefully constructed world collapsing

around her. Timothy's words hung in the air like a thunderclap, the truth of her identity exposed with such innocent candour that she couldn't even fault him for it. Her gaze fixed on Edward's face, watching as confusion gave way to understanding, then something deeper she couldn't quite name.

The small sitting room seemed to shrink further. She gripped the armrests of her chair, bracing herself for the rejection that would surely follow. After all, what vicar would want a fugitive from an orphanage —a liar who had deceived an entire village—associated with his parish?

"Reverend Thomas Sinclair," Edward repeated softly, his eyes never leaving Annabelle's face.

Timothy glanced between them, suddenly aware of his misstep. "I'm sorry, Belle. I didn't realise—"

"It's all right," Annabelle whispered, though nothing felt right at all. Her secret—the one thing that had protected her all these months—lay shattered on the floor between them.

Edward leaned forward, elbows on his knees, fingers steepled beneath his chin. The silence stretched unbearably until he finally spoke.

"I said I would help you, Annabelle, and that hasn't changed."

She blinked, certain she'd misheard him. "But I've lied to you—to everyone. I'm not Miss Smith. I'm a fugitive. There are notices in the village square with my description."

"I know who you are now," Edward said, his voice steady and sure. "You're the daughter of a vicar, a gifted teacher who has transformed the lives of children in this village, and a woman of remarkable courage who survived circumstances that would break most people."

Annabelle felt tears prickling behind her eyes, unexpected and unwelcome.

"The details of your past may have changed," Edward continued, "but the person I've come to know these past months—that hasn't changed at all."

51
ACCEPTANCE

Annabelle couldn't quite believe Edward's words. The acceptance in his eyes seemed genuine, yet experience had taught her that safety could vanish in an instant. She glanced at Timothy, whose expression had darkened since his accidental revelation.

"There's more you should know," Timothy said, his voice dropping to just above a whisper. "Those notices in the square—they're not just here. They've spread across three counties now."

Annabelle's breath caught. "Three counties?"

Timothy nodded grimly. "The search has only intensified. I've seen your description posted in every market town between Liverpool and here."

Edward frowned. "But why such effort for one escaped girl? Surely there are others who—"

"It's not just about her escape," Timothy interrupted, leaning forward. "It's about who's looking for her."

Annabelle felt a chill creep up her spine. "Who?"

"That vicar who replaced your father—Bloom. He's made

quite a name for himself since you left." Timothy's eyes hardened. "He's become a close advisor to some bishop. Harrington, I think the name was."

The room seemed to tilt beneath Annabelle. Her fingers dug into the worn fabric of the armchair.

"Bishop Harrington?" Edward's voice sounded distant to her ears. "The same Bishop Harrington who's visiting our parish soon?"

Timothy nodded. "That's the one. I overheard them in an inn near Blackburn. They were asking specifically about a red-haired girl who'd escaped from Thornfield. Said she was dangerous—claimed she'd attacked a carriage driver."

Annabelle's mind raced. The connection between Bloom and the Bishop explained everything—the plagiarised treatise, the seemingly never-ending search, the timing of the notices appearing just before the Bishop's visit.

"They seemed desperate to find you, Belle," Timothy continued. "Bloom especially. Something about papers that belonged to your father. I'm sure he wanted to keep the search subtle at first, he wouldn't want to draw any unwanted attention. But I've seen the notices about you. They're getting desperate and scared."

The manuscripts. The theological notes that Bloom had taken from her father's study after his death—the same ideas she'd recognised in Bishop Harrington's treatise. Her father's life's work, stolen and claimed by others. And she was the only one who would know.

Annabelle's hands trembled. The sanctuary she'd found in Meadowbrook was crumbling around her, and the Bishop who might destroy everything was arriving in less than two weeks.

Annabelle watched Edward's expression shift as Timothy's words settled between them. His brow furrowed, eyes narrowing slightly as though examining a difficult passage of scripture. She recognised that look—the same concentrated gaze he wore when working through theological problems in their discussions.

"Your father was Thomas Sinclair," Edward said slowly, almost to himself. "From St Michael's parish in Somerset?"

Annabelle nodded, her throat tight.

Edward's fingers drummed against his knee. "I've read passages from his sermons in seminary. They were... remarkable." His eyes widened suddenly. "And the treatise—Harrington's treatise on divine providence that I showed you—"

"Contains my father's ideas," Annabelle finished quietly. "His exact phrasings in some parts."

Edward stood abruptly, pacing the small room. "The section on suffering as refinement, not punishment—that was your father's concept, wasn't it? And the passage about divine timing manifesting through human choice..." He stopped, turning to face her. "I always thought those concepts felt different from Harrington's usual style. More intimate, somehow. More..."

"Human," Annabelle supplied. "My father believed theology should comfort the afflicted, not just instruct the faithful."

Edward's face had drained of colour. "All this time, I've been praising Harrington's brilliance to you, and they were your father's words." He sank back into his chair, looking ill. "How many other ideas has he claimed? How much of his reputation is built on stolen work?"

Annabelle felt a strange calm settle over her. For years, she'd carried her father's Bible as his only legacy. Now, his ideas lived on—twisted and uncredited, but alive nonetheless.

"Bloom must have taken the manuscripts after Father died," she said. "I saw him sorting through Father's papers before I was sent to Thornfield. He kept setting certain pages aside."

Edward's jaw tightened. "And now Bishop Harrington comes to evaluate me based on how well I implement principles that were never his to begin with.

"This is unconscionable," he said, his voice low but vibrating with intensity. "A man of the cloth—a bishop—building his reputation on the work of a deceased vicar who can no longer defend himself or receive credit."

Annabelle felt a curious warmth spread through her chest despite the gravity of their situation. No one had championed her father's memory this way since his death.

"Your father's ideas weren't just clever theological musings, Annabelle. They offered genuine comfort to people struggling with their faith." Edward stopped pacing and faced her directly. "I've seen parishioners weep with relief when I've shared those concepts from Harrington's—no, from your father's work."

Timothy, who had been silent, leaned forward. "I never knew your father was so important, Belle." His voice carried a newfound reverence. "All those times you read to me from his Bible, taught me his words... I didn't understand what it meant beyond our little world at Thornfield."

Edward nodded. "Reverend Sinclair's approach to divine providence brought comfort to countless souls. And now his daughter sits before us, pursued by the very men who stole his legacy." His hands clenched into fists. "I cannot stand by and allow this injustice to continue."

The intensity of Edward's gaze made Annabelle's breath catch. This wasn't merely the concern of a vicar for his parishioner, nor even the affection of a man for a woman. This was something deeper—a recognition of a wrong that demanded to be righted.

"I'll help you, Belle," Timothy said firmly. "Whatever we need to do."

Edward nodded. "As will I. Bishop Harrington arrives in less than a fortnight. We must be prepared." He knelt before Annabelle's chair, his eyes level with hers. "Your father's work deserves recognition. And you deserve to live without fear. I promise you, Annabelle Sinclair, we will find a way to ensure both."

52
EDWARD'S VENTURE

Edward paced the length of his study, gathering papers with a methodical precision that belied the tumult within. The decision to journey to St Michael's parish weighed upon him—not for the distance, but for what might be unearthed there. Annabelle's revelation about her father's theological writings and Bishop Harrington's suspicious acquisition of them demanded investigation.

"Parish management techniques," he muttered to himself, testing how the words sounded. A reasonable pretext, and one that sparked genuine interest. After all, hadn't he often wondered how other vicars maintained their parishes while pursuing scholarly work?

He folded a clean shirt and placed it in his travelling case alongside a small notebook bound in brown leather. His fingers lingered on the empty pages—what truths would fill them by journey's end? The thought of Annabelle's father, labouring over profound theological insights only to have them stolen after his death, kindled a righteous anger Edward rarely permitted himself.

"Reverend? Have you a moment?"

Edward looked up to find Mrs Hadley at his study door, a basket of freshly baked bread in her basket.

"I've brought provisions for your journey. The road to Somerset is long, and inn fare often leaves much to be desired."

"Your kindness overwhelms me, Mrs Hadley." Edward accepted the basket, the warm scent of sourdough rising between them. "I shan't be gone above six days. Back well before the Bishop arrives."

"The parish will miss you, brief though your absence may be."

"This journey," Edward said, meeting her gaze directly, "is important for Meadowbrook's future. Trust that I undertake it with the parish's best interests at heart."

After she departed, Edward returned to his packing.

"Six days," he promised the empty room. "Six days to find the truth."

EDWARD STOOD before St Michael's parish church, the weathered stone façade exactly as Annabelle had described it. The afternoon sun cast long shadows across the churchyard where Reverend Sinclair now lay buried beside his beloved wife. Edward removed his hat, allowing the significance of the moment to settle upon him. This wasn't merely a church—it was the foundation of Annabelle's childhood, the place where her father had poured out his heart in service to his congregation.

"For you, Annabelle," he whispered, "and for your father's legacy."

The vicarage stood adjacent to the church, its windows reflecting golden sunlight. Edward pictured a young Annabelle running through the garden that now lay somewhat neglected, the rosebushes her mother had tended growing wild without her careful hand. His chest tightened at the thought of all she had lost.

Edward made his way through the village, observing the easy familiarity between shopkeepers and customers. A baker called out to a passing farmer by name, inquiring after his wife's health. Two elderly women paused their conversation to nod respectfully at Edward's clerical collar. This was the community that had embraced the Sinclairs that had witnessed Annabelle's grief and then her departure.

"Good afternoon," called a voice. "You must be Reverend Woolworth from Meadowbrook."

Edward turned to find a round-faced man approaching with an outstretched hand.

"Indeed I am. And you must be Mr Penrose."

"At your service." The parish administrator pumped Edward's hand enthusiastically. "We don't often receive visitors from parishes as far as Meadowbrook. What brings you to our humble St Michael's?"

Edward fell into step beside him. "I'm studying various approaches to parish management. Meadowbrook is growing, and I'm keen to establish systems that will serve us well into the future."

"A forward-thinking approach! Reverend Bloom speaks highly of the importance of proper documentation."

Edward kept his expression neutral at the mention of Bloom. "I understand St Michael's has maintained meticulous records over the years."

"Oh, indeed!" Penrose beamed with pride. "Dating back nearly a century. Reverend Sinclair—God rest his soul—was particularly thorough. His notes on parish affairs were most comprehensive."

"I'd be fascinated to see such exemplary record-keeping."

"Would you? Splendid! I've an hour before evening prayers. Let me show you our archives." Penrose gestured toward the church. "We keep everything in the vestry annex—perfectly organised, if I do say so myself."

Edward followed, heart quickening. "That's most kind of you, Mr Penrose. I'm particularly interested in how theological reflections are incorporated into parish documentation."

"Then you're in for a treat," Penrose said, unlocking the vestry door. "Reverend Sinclair's theological notes were quite remarkable. Though I must say, many of the most profound ones seem to have gone missing after his passing."

Edward followed Penrose into the vestry annex, a narrow chamber lined with bookshelves that sagged beneath the weight of leather-bound volumes and yellowing papers. The musty scent of aged parchment mingled with lingering traces of incense, creating an atmosphere both scholarly and sacred. A single window, its glass clouded with years of dust, cast weak light across the wooden table at the room's center.

"Everything is organised by year," Penrose explained, running his fingers along the spines of several ledgers. "Parish accounts to the left, correspondence in the center, and sermon notes and theological writings to the right."

Edward's pulse quickened as he approached the rightmost shelves. "And Reverend Sinclair's materials would be here?"

"What remains of them, yes." Penrose pulled out a leather folder. "He was quite brilliant, you know. Not the sort to command a room like our current Reverend Bloom, but his sermons had substance. The parishioners still speak of how he could explain complex theological concepts so simply that even the children understood."

Edward carefully opened the folder, finding neatly catalogued sermon notes. "He sounds like a remarkable man."

"Indeed. His death came as such a shock—barely six months after his wife passed. The poor child, left all alone." Penrose shook his head. "I sometimes wonder what became of little Annabelle."

Edward kept his expression neutral, though his heart hammered against his ribs. "The daughter, you mean?"

"Yes. Bright little thing with her mother's copper curls. Reverend Bloom arranged for her to be sent to Thornfield Orphanage after her father's passing. Said it would provide structure." Penrose frowned slightly. "Never sat right with some of us, but what could we do?"

Edward leafed through the papers, scanning dates and titles. "These sermons seem to reference additional theological writings."

"Ah, you've noticed that too?" Penrose leaned closer. "Reverend Sinclair maintained separate notebooks for his theological explorations. Quite innovative ideas about divine providence and the nature of faith. He would reference them in his sermons but kept the full manuscripts private until they were properly developed."

"And these manuscripts?" Edward asked, struggling to keep his voice even.

"That's the peculiar thing." Penrose pulled out a parish inventory ledger, flipping to an entry dated shortly after Reverend Sinclair's death. "According to this, there were three bound volumes of theological notes and several loose manuscripts among Reverend Sinclair's personal effects. But look here—" He pointed to a notation in different ink. "All listed as 'missing' during the transition to Reverend Bloom's tenure."

Edward stared at the inventory, his suspicions crystallising into certainty. The notation was dated precisely three days after Reverend Sinclair's funeral—the very day Annabelle had overheard Bloom arranging to send her to Thornfield.

"Most unfortunate," Edward murmured, lodging the evidence in his memory. "Were inquiries made about their disappearance?"

"Reverend Bloom suggested they were likely of little value—preliminary thoughts rather than finished work."

Edward closed the inventory ledger with trembling fingers, a surge of righteous anger coursing through him. The evidence before him confirmed what Annabelle had suspected—her father's theological writings hadn't simply disappeared; they'd been deliberately taken. And now those same ideas were being proclaimed as Bishop Harrington's own brilliant insights.

"Mr Penrose, might I make copies of these inventory records?" Edward asked, keeping his voice steady despite his racing heart. "They provide an excellent example of thorough documentation."

"Of course, Reverend Woolworth." Penrose pulled out a sheet of parchment. "Use my desk. I'll fetch fresh ink."

While Penrose busied himself, Edward swiftly copied the damning entries, noting dates and specific descriptions of Reverend Sinclair's missing manuscripts. He also transcribed several sermon references that clearly pointed to theological concepts now featured prominently in Harrington's published work.

"I cannot thank you enough for your assistance," Edward said, folding the papers and tucking them securely inside his coat pocket. "St Michael's record-keeping will certainly serve as a model for Meadowbrook."

"Delighted to be of service," Penrose replied, walking Edward to the vestry door. "Will you be staying for evening prayers?"

Edward shook his head, already calculating the fastest route back to Meadowbrook. "I'm afraid I must depart immediately. Parish duties await."

He bid farewell to Penrose with a firm handshake, striding purposefully toward the stables where he'd left his horse. The afternoon sun had begun its descent, casting long shadows across the churchyard. Edward paused briefly beside Thomas Sinclair's grave, placing his hand upon the cool stone.

"I will help her reclaim what was taken," he whispered. "Your words will not be silenced."

Mounting his horse, Edward turned toward the road that would lead him back to Meadowbrook—back to Annabelle. The thought of her waiting for his return filled him with renewed determination. This wasn't merely about exposing a theological theft; it was about restoring dignity to a man whose final legacy had been stolen, and protecting the daughter who had already lost so much.

As he rode, Edward reflected on how deeply Annabelle had come to matter to him. Her courage, her resilience, her unwavering commitment to truth—these qualities had captured his heart long before he'd known her true identity. Now, understanding the full measure of what she had endured only strengthened his admiration.

"We'll face this together," he murmured as his horse cantered steadily eastward. The evidence secured against his chest felt like a shield—the first step toward justice. With Timothy's testimony and Annabelle's knowledge of her father's work, they now had a chance to challenge the powerful men who had wronged her family.

53
ARREST

Annabelle stood frozen beside a stall of spring vegetables, her wicker basket half-filled with carrots and potatoes. The market day bustle had been comforting until now—familiar faces haggling good-naturedly, children weaving between stalls, the smell of fresh bread from the baker's cart. She'd almost forgotten the notices posted at the town hall, almost believed she might truly belong here.

Mrs Fallington's voice shattered that illusion like a stone through glass.

"I have proof!" Mrs Fallington declared, her silk dress rustling as she pushed through the crowd toward Annabelle. She clutched a paper in her gloved hand, waving it like a battle flag. "This woman is not who she claims to be!"

The market chatter died. Dozens of eyes turned toward Annabelle.

"You're nothing but a fugitive!" Mrs Fallington's accusation rang across the square. "This is the red-haired girl who escaped from Thornfield Orphanage. The very same who assaulted a carriage driver and fled justice!"

Annabelle's basket slipped from nerveless fingers. Carrots scattered across the cobblestones. The world seemed to tilt beneath her feet as blood rushed in her ears.

"They're offering ten pounds for information leading to her capture," Mrs Fallington continued, her voice dripping with righteous indignation. "She's been deceiving us all—living amongst decent folk while authorities search for her, a criminal!"

The villagers' faces blurred before Annabelle's eyes. Mrs Hadley, who'd given her fresh bread every Sunday. Mr Fletcher, whose son she'd taught to read. All staring with expressions shifting from confusion to suspicion.

"Is it true?" someone called from the crowd.

"Red hair, educated speech—it fits," muttered another.

"A fugitive teaching our children?" gasped a mother, pulling her daughter closer.

Annabelle's throat closed. The accusations hung in the air, undeniable and damning. Seven years at Thornfield, the escape with Timothy, the life she'd built here—all collapsing around her like a house of cards. Her legs trembled beneath her skirt. She'd known this day might come, but nothing had prepared her for the overwhelming humiliation of being exposed before the entire village.

"That's quite enough, Mrs Fallington."

Miss Chilton's voice cut through the murmurs as she stepped between Annabelle and her accuser. Though shorter than Mrs Fallington, Miss Chilton somehow seemed to tower over her.

"Whatever Miss Smith—or Miss Sinclair—may have done before arriving in Meadowbrook, she has served this village and its children with nothing but dedication and kindness."

"The law—" Mrs Fallington began.

"The law?" Miss Chilton's laugh held no humour. "The law

that sends orphaned children to orphanages and workhouses where they're treated worse than animals? The law that would have sent this gifted teacher to Thatchwood Mill, where girls return broken or not at all?"

Miss Chilton turned, addressing the gathered villagers directly. "I knew Annabelle's circumstances when I took her in. Every one of us deserves a second chance to rebuild our lives. Would any of you truly see her punished for seeking a better life than the one thrust upon her?"

Annabelle watched the villagers' faces as Miss Chilton defended her. Some softened at the schoolmistress's words, but others hardened with disapproval. Mrs Fallington's triumphant expression told Annabelle everything she needed to know—the damage was done.

"A criminal teaching our children cannot stand," Mrs Fallington announced, turning toward Mr Thorne, who served as magistrate for Meadowbrook. "Surely you agree, sir?"

Mr Thorne shifted uncomfortably, his weathered face troubled. "This is a serious matter that requires proper consideration."

Within hours, word spread through the village like wildfire. Annabelle sat in Miss Chilton's cottage. Outside, she could hear the murmurs growing louder as villagers gathered, discussing her fate.

By evening, Mr Thorne arrived with two parish constables. His expression was grave as he removed his hat.

"Miss Sinclair, an emergency meeting of the parish council has been called. I'm afraid I must detain you pending investigation into these allegations."

Miss Chilton protested vigorously, but the order had been signed. Annabelle would be held in the small room behind the magistrate's office until representatives from Thornfield could arrive to identify her.

"I'm sorry," Mr Thorn said quietly. "The law must take its course."

As the constables escorted her across the village square, Annabelle felt the weight of stares pressing down upon her. Dark clouds gathered overhead, matching her spirits. The freedom she'd fought so desperately to achieve was slipping away like water through cupped hands.

Her mind raced with bitter thoughts. All her careful work, her teaching, her connections with the children—none of it mattered now. She was once again defined solely by her status: fugitive. The room they led her to was clean but sparse, with a narrow cot and barred window. Not unlike Thornfield, she thought grimly.

Through the window, Annabelle heard a commotion outside. Timothy's voice carried above the crowd.

"It was me who assaulted the driver! Annabelle had no choice but to flee!"

She rushed to the window. Timothy stood in the market square, addressing the gathered villagers with his hands raised.

"I knocked the driver unconscious and forced her to escape with me," he continued, his voice ringing with conviction. "She's innocent of any wrongdoing. If someone must be punished, let it be me alone!"

Annabelle pressed her hands against the cold bars, horror washing over her as Timothy sacrificed himself to protect her.

Annabelle pressed her face against the cold iron bars, watching in horror as Timothy stood defiantly in the village square. The crowd had fallen silent, hanging on his every word as he claimed full responsibility for the assault on the carriage driver. His shoulders were squared, chin lifted—the same stubborn stance she'd seen countless times at Thornfield when he'd defended younger children from bullies.

"I acted alone!" Timothy's voice carried across the square. "Annabelle had no choice but to flee or be sent back to face punishment for something she didn't do!"

The villagers exchanged uncertain glances. Annabelle could read their expressions—confusion, doubt, reluctant admiration for Timothy's courage. Mrs Fallington's face had gone rigid with frustration as her perfect accusation began to unravel.

Mr Thorne stepped forward, his brow furrowed. "Young man, are you confessing to assaulting the Thornfield carriage driver?"

"I am," Timothy answered without hesitation. "I knocked him unconscious and told Annabelle to run. She'd have been sent to Thatchwood Mill otherwise—no better than a death sentence."

The constables moved toward Timothy, heavy boots scraping against cobblestones. Annabelle's heart hammered against her ribs. She wanted to scream, to tell them it wasn't true—that they'd both planned the escape together. But the words stuck in her throat as she watched Timothy willingly sacrifice his freedom for hers.

As the constables flanked him, Timothy's eyes found hers through the barred window. A ghost of his familiar smile crossed his face.

"You must stay strong. I'll figure this out!" he called, his voice dropping to a fierce whisper that somehow carried to her ears alone.

Before the constables could lead him away, Timothy reached inside his coat. Annabelle held her breath, terrified he might do something rash, but he pulled out only a crumpled, yellowed paper. He thrust it toward Miss Chilton, who stood nearby.

"For Annabelle," he insisted. "This letter—I found it among

Pullter's papers while planning our escape. It proves Vicar Bloom arranged to have her sent away to silence her. Pullter was paid to do it."

Miss Chilton took the letter, her expression grave as she nodded.

The constables gripped Timothy's arms, but he didn't resist. "It's your proof," he called to Annabelle. "Your chance to clear your name."

Annabelle watched helplessly as Timothy was led away, his back straight despite the constables' firm grip on his arms. The crowd parted before them like water around stones, their faces a blur of curiosity and judgment. Timothy didn't look back again, but his final words echoed in her mind: "Your chance to clear your name."

Mr Thorne approached her cell, keys jangling at his belt. His weathered face showed lines of concern as he unlocked the door.

"Miss Sinclair," he said quietly, "I'm releasing you into Miss Chilton's custody until this matter is resolved. Don't leave the village."

Annabelle stepped out, legs unsteady. "But Timothy—"

"The young man confessed freely," Mr Thorne replied. "I cannot release him without proper investigation."

The village square that had once welcomed her now felt hostile. Whispers followed her as she crossed the cobblestones. Children who had once eagerly raised their hands in her classroom now hid behind their mothers' skirt. The baker who had praised her patience with his son now averted his eyes.

Annabelle blinked rapidly, fighting tears that threatened to spill. She would not give Mrs Fallington the satisfaction of seeing her break. Timothy had sacrificed his freedom for hers

—the least she could do was remain strong enough to use the gift he'd given her.

Miss Chilton appeared at her side, a steadying hand on her elbow. "Come, my dear. We have work to do."

Annabelle nodded, her resolve hardening like iron in a forge. Edward would return soon with evidence of the Bishop's theft. Combined with Timothy's letter, perhaps they could expose the truth before it was too late.

She turned her gaze toward the road leading out of Meadowbrook—the road Edward had taken days ago. "Please hurry," she whispered, the prayer carried away by the wind.

54
THE LETTER

Annabelle paced the small confines of Miss Chilton's sitting room, the letter from Timothy clutched tightly in her hand. She had read it three times already, each reading confirming what she had suspected—Reverend Bloom had orchestrated her removal to Thornfield specifically to keep her quiet about her father's theological writings. The evidence was there in black and white, in Bloom's own handwriting to Mr. Pullter, arranging payment for her immediate transfer after her father's death.

"He stole everything," she whispered, her voice catching. "My home, my father's work, my future."

Miss Chilton glanced up from her mending. "Perhaps you should rest, Annabelle. You've had quite an ordeal."

But rest was impossible. Every time Annabelle closed her eyes, she saw Timothy being led away by the constables, his shoulders squared with defiance despite the heavy burden he carried for her sake. She moved to the window instead, watching the road for any sign of Edward's return.

The afternoon sun cast long shadows across Meadowbrook's main street when Annabelle finally spotted a familiar figure on horseback. Edward's normally immaculate appearance was disheveled, his hair windblown and his clerical clothes creased from hard riding. Even from a distance, she could see the urgency in his posture as he leaned forward in the saddle, urging his mount faster toward the village.

Annabelle's heart quickened. He was back—but did he bring the proof they needed?

She watched as Edward pulled his horse to an abrupt halt outside the church. A small group of parishioners approached him immediately, their gestures animated. Edward's expression shifted from determination to shock as they spoke. His shoulders sagged visibly, and he dismounted with none of his usual grace, nearly stumbling as his boots hit the ground.

Someone was pointing toward the constable's office. Timothy.

Edward's gaze swept across the village square until it found Miss Chilton's cottage. Even across the distance, Annabelle felt the intensity of his eyes meeting hers at the window. Without hesitation, he strode toward the cottage, his long legs eating up the distance with purposeful strides.

Annabelle stepped back from the window, her fingers trembling as she smoothed her skirt. The letter crinkled in her hand—their evidence, their hope.

The cottage door swung open with such force that Miss Chilton's teacup rattled on its saucer. Edward stood in the doorway, his face flushed from exertion, hair dishevelled by wind and worry.

"They've taken Timothy," Annabelle said before he could speak, her voice barely steady. "He confessed to attacking the driver, though we both know it was him protecting me. And this—" She thrust the letter toward Edward. "Timothy found it among Pullter's papers. Proof that Bloom arranged my transfer to Thornfield immediately after discovering my father's manuscripts."

Edward crossed the room in three long strides, taking the letter with one hand and grasping Annabelle's trembling fingers with the other.

"I found more," he said, his voice low and urgent. "Parish records at St Michael's show your father's theological manuscripts were catalogued after his death but disappeared during Bloom's first month as vicar." He reached inside his coat and withdrew several folded papers. "The inventory matches passages in Harrington's treatise—word for word in some cases."

Annabelle sank into a chair, the weight of confirmation pressing against her chest. "They've stolen everything from me—my home, my father's legacy. And now Timothy..." Her voice broke.

Edward knelt before her, his blue eyes meeting hers with unwavering intensity. "I promise to help both of you. I've learned enough to confront Harrington, and together we can expose the truth about what Bloom did." His eyes shone with conviction, reaching deep into Annabelle's heart, igniting a spark of hope amid her distress.

"But I'm just a fugitive," she whispered. "Who would believe me against a bishop?"

"The truth will speak for itself," Edward said firmly, taking both her hands in his. "Timothy risked everything because he believes in you. His sacrifice would be meaningless if you abandon the fight now." He squeezed her hands gently. "You survived Thornfield. You built a new life here through your own courage and intelligence. Don't let them take that from you as well."

Miss Chilton stepped forward, placing a supportive hand

on Annabelle's shoulder. "He's right, my dear. You're stronger than you know."

Annabelle straightened her shoulders, feeling something of her father's resolve stirring within her. Perhaps Edward was right. Perhaps there was strength in their unity that neither Bloom nor Harrington could overcome.

55
PREPARATION

Annabelle stood by the window of Miss Chilton's cottage, watching as two horsemen galloped into the village. The riders wore the distinctive uniform of the diocese, their urgent pace suggesting important news. Her stomach tightened into a knot as she recognized the significance—Bishop Harrington's arrival was imminent.

"They're here," she called over her shoulder to Edward, who was examining the parish records spread across the table.

Edward joined her at the window, his presence solid and reassuring beside her. "Advance messengers. The Bishop himself will likely arrive tomorrow."

Annabelle's hands trembled slightly as she smoothed her skirt. "So soon? I thought we'd have more time to prepare."

"Perhaps it's better this way," Edward said, his voice low and determined. "Less time for doubt to creep in."

The weight of Timothy's sacrifice pressed heavily on Annabelle's heart. Each hour he spent in that cell was an hour too many, all because he had protected her. She couldn't fail him now.

Edward gathered the documents from the table, carefully arranging them in a leather portfolio. "We need to be strategic about this visit. We can't let him or Bloom intimidate us."

"What if they deny everything?" Annabelle asked, voicing the fear that had been growing inside her. "A bishop's word against mine—a fugitive."

"That's why we have these," Edward tapped the portfolio containing the evidence. "And why we need to choose our moment carefully. The Sunday service would give us witnesses—respectable members of the parish who would hear our case."

Annabelle nodded slowly, remembering her father's words about truth being God's language.

They spent the afternoon formulating their approach, anticipating objections, rehearsing what to say.

As dusk fell across Meadowbrook, Annabelle felt a curious blend of dread and determination. The coming confrontation would determine not just her future, but Timothy's freedom and her father's legacy.

"Are you afraid?" she asked Edward quietly.

"Yes," he admitted without hesitation. "But not enough to stop." He reached across the table and briefly squeezed her hand. "We'll face this together."

56
THE BISHOP'S ARRIVAL

Annabelle smoothed her plain grey dress, the most respectable garment she owned, as the church bells of St Matthew's rang out across Meadowbrook. From Miss Chilton's window, she watched villagers stream toward the square, their Sunday best giving the humble village an air of festivity. Bishop Harrington's carriage was expected within the hour.

"Ready?" Miss Chilton appeared at her door, her own dress pressed for the occasion.

Annabelle nodded, though her throat felt tight. She tucked her father's Bible into her bag, its familiar weight against her hip a reminder of why she must face this day with courage.

The village square had transformed overnight. Garlands of summer flowers draped across the church entrance, and the parish hall gleamed from a hasty scrubbing. Mrs Fallington directed a group of women arranging refreshments, her daughter Clara hovering nearby in a pale blue dress that caught the morning light.

Annabelle kept to the edges of the gathering crowd, aware

of the whispers that stood behind her. The discovery of her true identity still rippled through Meadowbrook like stones cast in still water.

Edward stood at the church steps, collar crisp and face composed, though Annabelle recognised the tension in his shoulders. Their eyes met briefly across the crowd, and he gave her a small nod—their signal that nothing had changed in their plan. Tomorrow's service would be their moment.

A stir at the far end of the square announced the arrival. The crowd parted as an ornate carriage rolled to a stop before the church steps, the diocesan crest emblazoned on its polished door.

Bishop Darius Harrington emerged like a figure from another world. His elaborate robes of deep purple caught the sunlight, gold embroidery glinting at every fold. Tall and imposing, with a stern face framed by silver-streaked hair, he surveyed the village with the practiced gaze of a man accustomed to deference.

Behind him, a slighter figure emerged—Vicar Bloom, his familiar pinched face now adorned with an expression of smug satisfaction.

Edward stepped forward, bowing with perfect respect. "Bishop Harrington, welcome to Meadowbrook. We're honoured by your presence."

The Bishop's voice carried across the square as he clasped Edward's hand. "Reverend Woolworth. I've heard promising things about your work here."

Annabelle watched the exchange, her heart pounding against her ribs. Edward's face betrayed nothing of their plan as he led the Bishop toward the waiting villagers.

Annabelle shrank back as Vicar Bloom's gaze swept the crowd. She turned away, heart hammering against her ribs, and slipped behind a cluster of villagers. The familiar cold dread from her orphanage days crept up her spine. How easily he could point her out, expose her to the Bishop before they had gathered their evidence.

"Miss Sinclair." Mrs Fallington's voice cut through the murmuring crowd. She stood mere inches away, her mouth curved in a tight smile. "Or should I say, Miss Smith? I believe the Bishop would be most interested to meet you."

Annabelle's mouth went dry. "Mrs Fallington, please—"

"Mother," Clara tugged at her mother's sleeve, her voice low but sharp. "Not now."

Mrs Fallington's eyebrows arched in surprise at her daughter's intervention. She hesitated, then turned away with a huff, being led away by Clara.

Annabelle exhaled shakily, catching Miss Chilton's concerned glance from across the square. She gave a small nod to indicate she was all right.

The Bishop's entourage moved toward the parish house, Edward walking alongside him, shoulders straight, voice measured as he discussed the village's needs. Bloom trailed behind them, his thin frame rigid with importance.

As they disappeared inside, the villagers dispersed into smaller groups, voices buzzing with excitement about tomorrow's service. Annabelle remained where she was, one hand pressed against her father's Bible through the fabric of her bag.

"He didn't see me," she whispered to Miss Chilton as her friend approached.

"Good. Let's keep it that way until tomorrow." Miss Chilton squeezed her arm. "Come, we should return home. Too many curious eyes here."

As they walked away from the square, Annabelle glanced back at the parish house where her fate would be decided. Tomorrow, she would stand before the congregation with the truth. Tomorrow, she would face the men who had stolen her father's words and her childhood. Tomorrow, she would reclaim her name.

For tonight, though, she would prepare, reading her father's notes one final time, drawing strength from his wisdom and Timothy's sacrifice.

57
CONFRONTATION

Annabelle slipped into the church just as the bells ceased their tolling. The pews had filled quickly, with villagers dressed in their Sunday finest, necks craning to glimpse Bishop Harrington. She found her place beside Miss Chilton near the middle of the congregation, far enough from the front to avoid immediate notice yet close enough to hear every word.

The air felt thick with anticipation. Whispers rustled through the church like wind through summer wheat, dying down only when the vestry door opened. Edward emerged first, followed by Bishop Harrington in his elaborate vestments, and finally Vicar Bloom, whose thin lips curved into a self-satisfied smile.

Annabelle's fingers tightened into a fist, missing the familiar feeling of her Father's Bible in her hand. She had spent the night tracing his marginal notes, comparing them to the passages in Harrington's treatise. The evidence lay within these pages, waiting to be revealed. It now was safely held in Edward's, ready to be employed in his accusation.

Edward caught her eye briefly as he took his place at the front. His face remained composed, but she recognised the slight furrow between his brows—the same expression he wore when working through a difficult theological question. He stood tall, shoulders squared, as if bearing the weight of what was to come.

The congregation rose for the opening hymn. Annabelle's voice faltered on the familiar words, her throat tight with anxiety. Her palms dampened with sweat as she gripped the hymnal, and she found herself counting breaths to steady her racing heart.

After the opening prayers, Bishop Harrington stepped forward. His commanding presence filled the small country church as he began to speak, his voice resonating with practiced authority.

"Beloved in Christ," he intoned, "today I wish to speak to you about the virtues that form the foundation of our faith—humility, truth, and integrity."

Annabelle nearly flinched at the words. The irony of hearing about integrity from a man who had stolen her father's work burned in her chest like a hot coal. She glanced at Edward, whose jaw had tightened almost imperceptibly.

As the Bishop continued, expounding on the importance of honesty in Christian life, Edward's expression grew increasingly resolute. When finally the Bishop concluded and returned to his seat, Edward approached the pulpit with measured steps.

He paused, surveying the congregation with clear eyes before beginning in a voice that, though quiet, carried to every corner of the church.

"Today," Edward said, "I wish to speak about truth and justice—about the sacred nature of a person's words and ideas, and the grievous sin of taking what is not rightfully ours."

Edward's voice was steady yet charged with purpose. He held up parish records and her father's Bible side by side.

"These theological concepts on divine providence that Bishop Harrington has been praised for—they appear word for word in Reverend Thomas Sinclair's personal notes. Notes that mysteriously disappeared after his death, when Vicar Bloom took over St Michael's parish."

Gasps erupted throughout the congregation. Mrs Hadley clutched her chest while Mr Fletcher's mouth hung open in disbelief. Even Clara Fallington leaned forward, her eyes wide with shock.

"I have here," Edward continued, "the original parish inventory listing Reverend Sinclair's theological manuscripts—and the subsequent inventory showing their disappearance during Vicar Bloom's first month."

Bishop Harrington's face darkened to a deep crimson. He rose from his seat, vestments rustling with the abrupt movement.

"This is preposterous!" His voice boomed through the church. "How dare you level such accusations against me in my presence? You forget yourself, Reverend Woolworth!"

The Bishop's finger jabbed toward Edward like a weapon. "I will see your career ended for this slander. Your ambitions for educational reform? Destroyed. Your position in this parish? Forfeit. No church in England will have you when I am finished."

Annabelle's heart hammered against her ribs. Edward stood unflinching beneath the Bishop's rage, though she could see the cost of his courage in the tightness around his eyes.

Vicar Bloom shifted uncomfortably beside the Bishop, his gaze darting around the church until suddenly, it locked with

Annabelle's. A slow, calculating smile spread across his thin lips.

"Perhaps," Bloom announced, rising to his feet, "we should consider the source of these malicious claims. There—" he pointed directly at Annabelle, "sits the fugitive from Thornfield Orphanage! Annabelle Sinclair, who assaulted a carriage driver and fled justice. A criminal whose word counts for nothing!"

The church erupted in confused murmurs. Annabelle felt the weight of every stare, the judgment in their eyes threatening to crush her resolve. Miss Chilton gripped her arm in silent support, but despair washed over Annabelle like a cold tide.

Then, something unexpected happened within her. The fear that had been her constant companion since her parents' deaths began to recede. In its place rose a fierce, burning determination she hadn't felt since the day she'd jumped from that carriage with Timothy.

Annabelle rose from her seat, the weight of her parents' memories lifting her shoulders rather than burdening them. The church fell silent as she stepped into the centre aisle, her threadbare dress a stark contrast to the Bishop's ornate vestments. She felt Miss Chilton's encouraging nod behind her, but kept her eyes fixed ahead.

"I am Annabelle Sinclair," she declared, her voice steady despite the trembling in her hands. "Daughter of Reverend Thomas Sinclair of St Michael's parish. And I have earned my right to speak."

The congregation stared, mouths agape. Mrs Fallington's face contorted with indignation, while Clara watched with unexpected interest as Annabelle defiantly made her way down the aisle to the front. Edward's eyes shone with pride as he handed her father's bible over, gently placing his hand on hers, before stepping aside from the pulpit.

Annabelle turned to face the parishioners who had both welcomed and judged her.

"This Bible belonged to my father," she said, opening it carefully. The spine creaked in protest as she revealed pages filled with neat handwriting in the margins. "These are his thoughts, his meditations on scripture, written in his own hand over many years."

She held the Bible higher, her finger tracing along a passage marked with her father's distinctive script. "Here, he writes of divine providence working through human suffering—the very words that appear in Bishop Harrington's celebrated treatise."

Bishop Harrington's face flushed deeper, his knuckles whitening as he gripped the edge of his seat.

"But I have more." Annabelle withdrew Timothy's letter from her pocket, unfolding it with deliberate care. "This letter details how Vicar Bloom arranged for my removal to Thornfield Orphanage immediately after discovering my father's manuscripts."

Her voice gained strength as she read aloud: "'The girl is to be sent to Thornfield without delay. Her presence complicates matters, particularly regarding the late Reverend's theological notes which show considerable promise for publication. I've made arrangements with Mr Pullter to ensure she remains there indefinitely.'"

Vicar Bloom's face drained of colour. He half-rose from his seat, mouth opening to protest, but no words emerged.

"I was ten years old," Annabelle continued, her words cutting through the stunned silence. "My father had just died. And instead of protection, I received banishment—so that my father's words could be stolen and claimed by others."

Bishop Harrington's composure crumbled. The proud man who had entered the church with such authority now seemed to shrink before her eyes. His gaze darted between the faces of the parishioners, reading their shock and disapproval. The crowd that had once looked upon him with reverence now regarded him with suspicion.

The Bishop cleared his throat and straightened his vestments, a desperate attempt to reclaim his dignity.

"Perhaps," he said, his voice noticeably softer than before, "we have had a misunderstanding. I was, of course, deeply influenced by Reverend Sinclair's theological insights. I should have been more explicit about my... inspirations."

Annabelle's breath caught in her throat. She glanced at Edward, whose expression remained resolute.

Bishop Harrington stepped forward, hands clasped before him in a gesture that mimicked humility. "I propose a solution that benefits us all. In future editions of my treatise, I shall acknowledge my inspiration from Reverend Sinclair's work." His eyes narrowed slightly.

He paused, scanning the congregation before his gaze settled on Annabelle and Edward. "All I ask in return is your discretion regarding the... full extent of the similarities between my work and Reverend Sinclair's notes. This would only damage the church's standing, after all."

A collective gasp rippled through the congregation. Mrs Hadley's hand flew to her mouth. Mr Fletcher shook his head in disbelief. Even Mrs Fallington appeared scandalised, her lips pressed into a thin line of disapproval.

Annabelle felt a storm of emotions swirling within her. Timothy's freedom dangled before her like a lifeline. She thought of him sitting in a cell, having sacrificed his liberty for hers. With a single word, she could secure his release.

Yet her father's words echoed in her memory: "Truth may not always be comfortable, Annabelle, but it is always right."

She looked down at the Bible in her hands, at her father's

careful notations in the margins—years of thought and devotion reduced to a mere "inspiration" in the Bishop's proposed compromise.

Edward stepped closer to her, his presence steady and reassuring. His eyes met hers, filled with the same conflict she felt. The choice before them seemed impossible.

58
STANDING YOUR GROUND

Edward stepped forward, his shoulders squared beneath his clerical robes. The church fell silent, as if the very air had solidified around them. Edward's gaze never wavered from Bishop Harrington's face as he spoke.

"Full attribution or nothing will suffice. Reverend Sinclair's legacy deserves to be honoured and recognised."

His voice carried to every corner of the church, clear and unwavering. Annabelle's breath caught in her throat. She had expected compromise, perhaps even surrender in the face of such powerful opposition. Instead, Edward stood firm, refusing to bend before the Bishop's authority.

Bishop Harrington's face darkened. "You would risk your future in the church for this?" he asked, his voice low and dangerous.

"I would risk it for the truth," Edward replied simply.

Annabelle felt something warm unfurl in her chest. After years of being silenced and dismissed, someone was finally standing up for her father's work—for her family's honour.

A murmur rippled through the congregation. Mrs Fletcher

leaned toward her husband, whispering urgently. Mr Thorne, the magistrate, frowned thoughtfully, his eyes moving between the Bishop and Edward. Even Clara watched with an intensity that surprised Annabelle.

Annabelle watched in stunned silence as Mrs Hadley rose to her feet, her weathered hands smoothing down her Sunday best.

"Miss Smi- Sinclair has been nothing but virtuous since she arrived here," she declared, her voice quavering but determined. "Seen how she helps the little ones with their letters. That's not the behaviour of someone with darkness in their heart."

Before Annabelle could process this unexpected support, Mr Fletcher stood, hat clutched in his hands.

"My Tommy couldn't read a word before Miss—before Annabelle took him under her wing. Now he reads to us every night from the Bible. That's God's work, that is, no matter what name she uses."

One by one, villagers rose. Mr Thorne, the magistrate himself, cleared his throat and addressed the Bishop directly.

"Sir, I have to say, the evidence presented, though it does need further examination, does not paint a very *honest* picture."

Annabelle's vision blurred with tears. She blinked them back, hardly daring to believe what was happening. These people who had whispered about her just days ago were now standing in her defence.

Miss Chilton stepped into the centre aisle, her spine straight as a ruler. "Annabelle Sinclair has taught our children with patience and wisdom beyond her years. She has borne hardship that would break most spirits, yet remains kind and generous. We will all testify to her character."

Most astonishing of all was Clara Fallington, who rose

gracefully from beside her mother. Mrs Fallington tugged at her daughter's sleeve, but Clara shook her off.

"I have not always been kind to Miss Sinclair," Clara admitted, her voice carrying clearly through the church. "But I recognise integrity when I see it. And I see it now, in her and in Reverend Woolworth."

The Bishop's face had grown increasingly pale as more villagers voiced their support. Vicar Bloom leaned toward him, whispering urgently, but Harrington waved him away.

The support continued to build, a wave of righteous indignation sweeping through the church. Annabelle felt tears prick her eyes as she watched the people of Meadowbrook transform from suspicious neighbours to fierce defenders of truth.

Annabelle felt Edward's hand find hers, warm and steady. She squeezed it gratefully, overwhelmed by the wall of support that had materialised around them. After years of loneliness at Thornfield, of being no one, she had somehow become someone worth defending by the people of Meadowbrook.

59
JUSTICE

The Bishop tugged at his collar, a thin sheen of perspiration visible on his forehead despite the cool air in the church. Vicar Bloom leaned toward him again, but Harrington silenced him with a sharp gesture.

Annabelle could almost see the calculations running behind his eyes. Every moment the opposition grew, more villagers finding their courage in the wake of others. Even those who remained seated watched with open interest, no longer averting their gaze when Annabelle looked their way.

Bishop Harrington cleared his throat, the sound unnaturally loud in the expectant silence that had fallen over the congregation.

"This is... most irregular," he began, his voice lacking its earlier resonance. "However, I can see that this parish holds... strong opinions on the matter."

Annabelle held her breath. Edward's hand tightened around hers.

The Bishop straightened his shoulders, making one last attempt to salvage his dignity. "In the interest of Christian harmony, and upon further reflection of the materials presented, I will ensure that Reverend Sinclair receives full attribution in all future editions of my treatise."

A collective gasp rippled through the church.

"Furthermore," he continued, the words clearly difficult for him to speak, "appropriate compensation shall be arranged for both Miss Sinclair and Reverend Woolworth from the proceeds of future publications."

"And for yourself and Reverend Bloom?" Edward pressed.

"What could you possibly mean?" Bloom spoke up. His face had turned a bright shade of crimson.

"We are supposed to be men of God, gentlemen." Edward said coolly. "And deception is not of the Lord."

"Surely attribution and compensation is enough?" The Bishop cried out.

"Will that be enough for the Lord, Bishop?" Edward asked.

The Bishop opened his mouth, but nothing came out.

"You both know this must be brought to the attention of the Archbishop." Edward said.

Both men cried out, making noises that did not resemble words.

"It is the only just and honest way." Edward continued. "He shall judge for your transgressions against Miss Sinclair and against her father. And I pray you may find redemption in the eyes of our Lord."

"You are... correct." The Bishop said deflating.

A trear dropped from Bloom's eye, and he nodded.

"Will that satisfy you, Reverend Woolsworth?" The Bishop finally said.

"Almost."

"Almost!" The two men cried out in unison.

Edward motioned to Annabelle. "St Michael's will need a

new vicar. I say we shall let Annabelle have a say in who is elected."

"It's only right." Bloom said softly to the Bishop. The Bishop seemed lost in thought for a second, before nodding.

For a moment, nobody moved. Then Mr Fletcher's voice broke the silence.

"Three cheers for truth and justice!"

The church erupted. Villagers embraced one another, hands clapped backs, and voices rose in celebration. Miss Chilton wiped tears from her eyes, and even Mr Thorne was smiling broadly.

Annabelle stood stunned, unable to process what had just happened. After years of powerlessness, of having everything taken from her—her parents, her home, her identity—something had finally been returned. Her father's work would bear his name. His ideas would live on, acknowledged as his own.

A wave of relief washed over her so powerful that her knees nearly buckled. Edward's arm slipped around her waist, steadying her.

"We did it," he whispered, his voice thick with emotion.

60
MYSTERIOUS WAYS

Annabelle sat beside Miss Chilton in the parlour of the cottage, her fingers absently tracing the worn leather cover of her father's Bible. Though the morning's victory still hummed through her veins, anxiety gnawed at her thoughts. Timothy remained in the village gaol, paying the price for her freedom.

"More tea?" Miss Chilton asked, reaching for the pot.

Before Annabelle could answer, the front door rattled with an urgent knock. Edward burst in without waiting for an invitation, his clerical collar askew and his eyes bright with excitement.

"They're releasing him," he announced breathlessly. "Timothy—the charges have been dropped!"

Annabelle leapt to her feet, the Bible tumbling from her lap to the floor. "When? How?"

"Mr Thorne just told me. The magistrate received statements from several villagers, especially a certain Mr Penrose, confirming the Bishop's misconduct. They've determined there were 'extraordinary circumstances' surrounding your escape."

Edward's face split into a wide grin. "Timothy should be walking free within the hour."

A cry escaped Annabelle's lips—half laugh, half sob. Miss Chilton clasped her hands together in delight.

"Oh, my dear girl! What wonderful news!"

"We should go to meet him," Edward suggested, already moving toward the door.

They hurried through the village, Annabelle's heart pounding with each step. After everything they'd endured—the orphanage, their desperate escape, the long separation—Timothy would finally be free. Not just from imprisonment, but from the shadow of Thornfield that had followed them both.

The village church stood peaceful in the afternoon light, its doors thrown open to catch the summer breeze. Edward suggested they wait there, away from curious eyes. Annabelle paced the nave, her thoughts racing with plans for Timothy's future. Perhaps he could help with the school, or Edward might find him work at the parish.

The sound of footsteps on the gravel path made her turn. Timothy appeared in the doorway, his tall frame silhouetted against the sunlight. For a moment, he stood frozen, blinking as his eyes adjusted to the dimmer light inside. Then his gaze found Annabelle, and his face broke into that familiar wide grin she'd missed so dearly.

"Belle," he said, softly.

Annabelle rushed forward, throwing her arms around him. Edward joined them, and the three stood locked in a tight embrace, bound by shared hardship and loyalty that words could never fully express.

Annabelle stepped out of the church with Timothy and Edward, blinking as bright spring sunshine washed over them. The village of Meadowbrook spread before them, transformed in her eyes. No longer a place of hiding, but of possibility.

"I can hardly believe it," she whispered, her voice catching. "For so long, I've been looking over my shoulder, waiting for someone to recognise me."

Timothy squeezed her hand. "No more running, Belle."

The three friends walked slowly down the path, past the gravestones and into the village proper. Annabelle felt lighter with each step, as though she'd shed a heavy cloak she'd worn for years.

"Your father would be so proud," Edward said, his voice gentle. "Not just of your courage, but of how you've carried his teachings forward."

Annabelle nodded, throat tight with emotion. "I keep thinking of what he told me before he died—that I had my mother's strength. I never truly understood what that meant until now."

They paused at the village green, where children played under the watchful eyes of their mothers. Annabelle watched a small girl with copper curls chase a hoop across the grass.

"I've been thinking," Timothy said, breaking the comfortable silence. "About those reading circles you mentioned, Reverend. What if we expanded them? Not just for children, but for adults who never had the chance to learn?"

Edward's face brightened. "Like the dock workers you met in Liverpool?"

"Exactly. Men who could better their positions if only they could read contracts and ledgers."

Annabelle felt a surge of excitement. "We could use Father's approach—teaching through stories that resonate with their daily lives."

They continued walking, their conversation flowing freely with ideas. Annabelle suggested outdoor lessons when the weather permitted. Timothy described how he'd seen a travelling teacher use pictures to help sailors learn letters in Liverpool. Edward spoke of petitioning neighbouring parishes to adopt similar programmes.

Laughter bubbled up between them, unexpected and welcome. For the first time since her parents' deaths, Annabelle felt truly alive—not merely surviving, but building something meaningful.

"Look at us," Timothy chuckled, gesturing between them. "The vicar, the teacher, and the former runaway. Who would have thought we'd be planning the future of education in Meadowbrook?"

"God works in mysterious ways," Edward replied with a smile that warmed Annabelle to her core.

61

SHARED CONFESSIONS

Annabelle walked beside Edward through the meadow, the late afternoon sun gilding the wildflowers in shades of amber and gold. Her steps felt lighter than they had in years—perhaps since before her mother's illness. The weight of deception no longer pressed upon her shoulders; her true name had been restored, her father's work would be properly credited, and Timothy was free.

A letter had arrived that morning from London. Edward had read it aloud at breakfast, his voice steady but his eyes dancing with satisfaction. Reverend Bloom and Bishop Harrington had been summoned before the Archbishop of Canterbury himself. The evidence Edward had gathered had proven damning. Both men were defrocked—stripped of their clerical positions.

"They're working as scribes now," Edward had told her. "Copying others' words rather than stealing them."

Annabelle plucked a daisy from amongst the grass, twirling it between her fingers. She ought to feel triumphant, perhaps even vengeful, yet something else entirely filled her heart.

"I pray Bloom and Harrington find redemption," she murmured, surprising herself with the sincerity of the words. "And peace."

Edward glanced at her, eyebrows raised. "After everything they did to you?"

"Perhaps because of it." She tucked the daisy behind her ear. "I know what it is to rebuild a life from nothing. I wouldn't wish that journey on anyone, though I'm grateful for where mine has led."

They crested the small hill that overlooked the village. Meadowbrook lay before them, bathed in golden light.

"There's more news," Edward said. "St Michael's has a new vicar. Young fellow named Richardson. By all accounts, he's revitalizing your father's old parish."

Annabelle felt a curious warmth spread through her chest.

"Father would be pleased," she said softly. "He loved that place so."

A sense of peace settled over her—not the fragile, tentative kind she'd clutched at during her years at Thornfield, but something solid and true. Her father's parish was in good hands. His work would bear his name.

"It's beautiful here," she said, reaching down to brush her fingertips across the tops of tall grasses. "I never truly noticed before. I was always too busy watching for danger."

Edward nodded, his eyes taking in the rolling landscape. "That's what fear does—blinds us to the beauty surrounding us."

They followed a narrow path that wound through clusters of bluebells. Annabelle smiled at the sight, remembering the pressed flower in her Bible—Timothy's gift from their orphanage days. How far they had all come since then.

"The children will love having lessons out here when

summer arrives properly," she said. "We could bring slates and books, perhaps even—"

"Annabelle." Edward stopped walking, turning to face her. Something in his tone made her pause, her words falling away.

The breeze stirred his dark hair as he stood before her, sunlight catching in his blue eyes. He seemed to be gathering his courage, his chest rising with a deep breath.

"I need to tell you something," he began, his voice steady yet filled with emotion. "I've been falling for you, Annabelle. You're remarkable, and I can't keep pretending it doesn't matter. But if you have feelings for Timothy—"

Annabelle stared at Edward, stunned into silence. His words seemed to hover in the air between them, as tangible as the meadow flowers brushing against her skirt. Her heart thundered in her chest as his confession settled into her understanding. Edward Woolworth—the vicar, the man who had defended her, fought for her father's legacy—harboured feelings for her.

A kaleidoscope of memories tumbled through her mind: Edward's patient guidance with the children, his passionate defence of education for all, and the way his eyes lit up during their theological discussions. She recalled how he'd believed in her when others doubted, stood beside her when the village turned against her, and risked his position to help uncover the truth.

"Timothy?" she finally managed, the question in Edward's voice finally registering. The misunderstanding nearly made her laugh despite the gravity of the moment.

"Edward," she finally said, her voice trembling slightly. "Timothy and I are more like brother and sister. We've shared pain and struggle, but it's never been anything romantic." She took a steadying breath, gathering courage from the warmth in his eyes. "My heart belongs to you. I feel the same way," she added, her eyes sparkling with sincerity.

Relief washed across Edward's face, followed by joy that transformed his features. The change was beautiful to behold—like watching sunrise break across the horizon after the longest night. He stepped closer, then surprised her by dropping to one knee amidst the wildflowers. From his pocket, he produced a simple silver ring, its modest appearance belying the depth of meaning it carried.

"Then, may I have the honour of asking you to be my wife?" His voice was steady now, blue eyes gazing up at her with hope and love so pure it took her breath away.

Annabelle's hand flew to her mouth as tears sprang unbidden to her eyes. After years of loss and hardship, after believing happiness might forever remain beyond her grasp, here was a future brighter than any she had dared imagine. A sob of joy escaped her as she nodded emphatically.

"Yes! Yes, I will marry you, Edward!"

62
ENGAGEMENT

Annabelle could scarcely believe how quickly life had transformed. In the days following Edward's proposal, she found herself swept up in a whirlwind of joy unlike anything she'd known since childhood. The silver ring on her finger caught the light as she arranged books in the schoolroom, a constant reminder that her future now held promise rather than peril.

"What about here for the natural science section?" Edward asked, gesturing to shelves near the window where afternoon sunlight would illuminate specimens the children collected.

"Perfect," Annabelle replied, watching how his eyes crinkled when he smiled. "The light will help them see details in leaves and rocks."

They spent evenings sketching plans for expanding the school, their heads bent together over parchment at Miss Chilton's kitchen table. Their shared vision took shape with each conversation—a school where children of farmers would sit alongside those of merchants, where girls would learn alongside boys, where no child would be turned away for lack of means.

"We'll need more space eventually," Edward mused, his shoulder warm against hers.

"And more books," Annabelle added, thinking of the children at Thornfield who had never held one.

Timothy threw himself into their plans with characteristic enthusiasm, proudly discussing his role as caretaker of the new school.

"I'll build proper desks," he declared one afternoon as they walked through the village. "Not those rickety things at Thornfield that pinched your fingers, Annabelle. Solid oak that'll last generations."

"And a garden," Annabelle suggested, remembering her mother's roses. "The children could grow vegetables and learn about nature firsthand."

Timothy nodded eagerly. "I could teach them what I know about soil and growing seasons."

The village embraced their engagement with surprising warmth. When before there was judgement of the class divide, now there was only appreciation for virtuous love. Mrs Hadley presented Annabelle with a hand-embroidered tablecloth for her future home. Mr Fletcher offered timber from his woodlot for school improvements. Even Mrs Fallington, chastened by recent events, sent a basket of preserves with Clara, who delivered it with genuine congratulations.

Miss Chilton watched it all with quiet satisfaction, occasionally catching Annabelle's eye with a knowing smile that seemed to say: See what happens when you dare to hope?

Each night, Annabelle touched the pressed bluebell in her father's Bible, silently thanking her parents for the strength they'd given her. She had survived the darkest valleys to find herself here—surrounded by friendship, purpose, and love that promised to illuminate all her days to come.

63
NO LONGER ALONE

Annabelle stood before the small mirror in Miss Chilton's spare bedroom, hardly recognising the woman who gazed back. Her copper curls had been arranged with sprigs of lavender and baby's breath, framing her face like a halo. The dress—a gift from the village women who had pooled their resources—was simple cream muslin with delicate embroidery along the hem.

"Your mother would be so proud," Miss Chilton said, adjusting the flowers in Annabelle's hair.

Annabelle touched the worn Bible resting on the dressing table.

"I wish they could be here," Annabelle whispered. "My parents..."

"They are, dear. In ways that matter most."

The church bells of St Matthew's began to peal, sending birds scattering from the tower. Annabelle took a steadying breath. After years of keeping her head down at Thornfield, of fearing discovery in Meadowbrook, today she would walk proudly under her own name, claiming her place in the world not as Miss Smith the governess nor as the runaway girl, but as Annabelle Sinclair—soon to be Annabelle Woolworth.

Timothy waited at the bottom of the stairs, dressed in new clothes purchased with his first proper wages as the school's caretaker. His eyes widened at the sight of her.

"Blimey, Annabelle. You look like something from a storybook."

She laughed, the sound bright and clear. "And you look positively respectable, Timothy."

"Don't get used to it," he grinned, offering his arm. "Shall we, then? Edward's pacing a trench in front of the altar."

The walk to the church passed in a blur of sunlight and well-wishes. Villagers lined the lane, smiling and nodding. Mrs Fletcher dabbed her eyes with a handkerchief. Mr Thorne doffed his hat. Even Mrs Fallington offered a genuine smile, her daughter Clara beside her with a basket of rose petals.

At the church door, Timothy squeezed her hand. "Ready?"

Annabelle nodded, thinking of all the paths that had led her here—from the vicarage garden where her mother had taught her about pruning roses, to the cold dormitory at Thornfield, to the schoolroom where she'd found her purpose.

The doors opened. Sunlight streamed through the stained glass, painting the stone floor in jewel tones. And there at the altar stood Edward, his face illuminated with such joy that Annabelle's heart nearly burst with answering happiness.

Annabelle's heart fluttered as she moved down the aisle toward Edward. Timothy walked beside her, standing in place of the father she had lost. The familiar faces of Meadowbrook turned to watch her passage—faces that had once regarded her with suspicion now beamed with genuine warmth.

Edward's eyes never left hers as she approached. His gaze

held such tenderness that she felt wrapped in it, protected by it. When Timothy placed her hand in Edward's, the touch anchored her to this moment that once seemed impossible.

"Dearly beloved," began the visiting vicar from the neighboring parish.

Annabelle barely heard the traditional words that followed. The church where she had once hidden in shadows now embraced her in light. Edward's hands were warm around hers, his thumbs gently stroking her skin in small, reassuring circles.

When the time came for their vows, Edward spoke first, his voice clear and steady.

"Annabelle, I promise to cherish your strength and courage, to support your dreams as you have supported mine. I vow to stand beside you in truth, to help create the world we envision together, where knowledge and compassion flourish. Your heart has taught mine to hope again."

Tears pricked Annabelle's eyes as she spoke her own vows, words she had carefully chosen.

"Edward, I promise to walk with you in honesty and faith. You saw me when I was invisible, believed in me when I doubted myself. I vow to build our life with the same care you've shown in rebuilding mine. In you, I've found not just shelter, but home."

The vicar nodded, satisfied with their promises. "The rings, if you please."

Timothy stepped forward, producing two simple silver bands. Edward slid one onto Annabelle's finger, and she returned the gesture, her hands steadier than she'd expected.

"By the authority vested in me, I now pronounce you husband and wife."

Edward cupped her face with gentle hands and leaned forward. Their lips met in a kiss that felt like a beginning—soft and certain. The church erupted in applause and cheers, Timothy's voice the loudest among them.

As they turned to face the congregation as husband and wife, Annabelle felt the weight of her past finally lift. No longer a fugitive, no longer alone.

64
A NEW NORMAL

Annabelle stood at the schoolhouse door, watching children file in with books clutched to their chests. The autumn sun cast long shadows across the yard, gilding the scene in amber light. Six months had passed since her wedding day, and still she sometimes caught herself in moments of disbelief at how dramatically her life had been transformed.

"Good morning, Mrs Woolworth," called Tommy Fletcher, now twelve and reading well above his age. His progress never failed to fill her with quiet pride.

"Good morning, Tommy. I see you've brought back 'Robinson Crusoe'—did you enjoy it?"

"Ever so much! Though I wouldn't fancy being stranded like that myself."

Annabelle smiled, remembering nights at Thornfield when she and Timothy had whispered dreams of adventure beneath thin blankets. Some journeys, she had learned, required no ships or distant shores to be transformative.

Inside the schoolroom, Edward was already arranging slates at each desk. He looked up as she entered, his face brightening in that way that still made her heart skip. Together they had expanded the school, not just in size but in purpose. Children from three surrounding villages now attended, some walking miles each day for the opportunity.

"The package from London arrived," Edward said, gesturing to a parcel on her desk. "First edition, with your father's name where it belongs."

Annabelle unwrapped the brown paper with careful fingers. Inside lay a handsomely bound volume: "Reflections on Divine Providence" by Bishop Darius Harrington, with prominent acknowledgment of "the foundational theological framework developed by the late Reverend Thomas Sinclair of St. Michael's Parish."

Her fingers traced her father's name on the title page. "He would have been pleased," she whispered, "not for the recognition, but knowing his ideas might bring comfort to others."

Edward came to stand beside her, his hand warm against her shoulder. "The first proceeds arrived as well. Enough to sponsor three children from Thornfield to attend school here next term."

Annabelle's eyes filled with tears. In her mind's eye, she could see her father in his study, quill poised over parchment as he worked late into the night, his face illuminated by candlelight. How fitting that his words, once stolen, now returned to light the way for children trapped in darkness as she once had been.

"Timothy's nearly finished the new desks," Edward added. "Says they'll be sturdy enough to withstand even the most enthusiastic young scholars."

65
HOME AT LAST

Annabelle sat in the parlour of the vicarage, afternoon light streaming through the windows and catching the dust motes that danced in the air. Three-year-old Elizabeth nestled against her side, her copper curls—so like Annabelle's own—tumbling over her shoulders as she peered at the worn leather Bible open across their laps.

"This one, Mama," Elizabeth said, her small finger hovering over a passage in Psalms where her grandfather's handwriting filled the margin.

Annabelle felt a familiar tightness in her chest—not the constriction of fear she'd known for so many years, but the fullness of gratitude that sometimes overwhelmed her still. This Bible had been her lifeline in Thornfield's bleakest hours, and now it served as a bridge between her daughter and the grandfather she would never meet.

Timothy sat across from them in the armchair Edward usually occupied, whittling a small wooden bird. He looked up, catching Annabelle's eye with the same mischievous glint that had sustained her through seven years of hardship.

"She reads as quickly as you did," he remarked, setting aside his knife. "Soon she'll be teaching the other children."

Elizabeth traced the faded ink of Thomas Sinclair's handwriting with reverent care. "What does this say, Mama?"

Annabelle leaned closer, reading the words that had once sustained her through endless nights on a thin orphanage mattress. "'Even in darkness, light dawns for the upright,'" she translated. "Your grandfather wrote that after visiting a family who'd lost everything in a fire, yet they still opened their home to others."

Elizabeth nodded solemnly, as though absorbing wisdom far beyond her years. The Bible that had once been Annabelle's only possession now served as the cornerstone of their family's legacy—not merely of faith, but of perseverance through trials.

"Uncle Timothy, did you know my grandfather?" Elizabeth asked, turning her bright blue eyes—so like Annabelle's father's—toward him.

"I didn't have that honour," Timothy replied, setting his whittling aside to join them on the settee. "But your mother shared his words with me when we had nothing else."

Annabelle reached for Timothy's hand, squeezing it gently. What strange and wondrous providence had brought them here—from the cold dormitories of Thornfield to this warm parlour where love flowed freely. The vicarage that had once seemed forever lost to her was now her home again, though in a different village with a different name above the door.

Annabelle heard the front door open and close, followed by Edward's familiar footsteps in the hallway. Elizabeth's head lifted at the sound, her eyes brightening with recognition. The little girl scrambled from her mother's lap, nearly toppling the Bible in her haste.

"Papa's home!" she announced, as though it were a discovery of monumental importance.

Annabelle carefully closed the Bible, running her fingers over its worn cover before setting it aside. The book had journeyed with her through darkness into light, its pages a testament to all she had endured and overcome.

Edward appeared in the doorway, his clerical collar loosened after a day of parish duties. His face, which had once seemed impossibly handsome to Annabelle during those first days in Meadowbrook, had only grown dearer with the passing years. The lines at the corners of his eyes spoke of laughter shared, of burdens carried together.

"There are my favourite people," he said, scooping Elizabeth into his arms. She giggled as he planted a kiss on her forehead. "And what have you been studying today, my scholar?"

"Grandfather's Bible," Elizabeth replied importantly. "The part about light in darkness."

Edward's eyes met Annabelle's over their daughter's head, understanding passing between them without words needed. He crossed to where she sat and bent to kiss her, his lips warm against hers.

"And how are you today, Mrs Woolworth?" he asked softly.

"Grateful," Annabelle answered simply, for it was the truest word she knew.

Timothy rose from his chair, tucking his whittling knife into his pocket. "I'll leave you to your family supper. The new desks will be ready for Monday's lessons."

As Timothy took his leave, Annabelle watched her husband settle into the chair with their daughter, listening intently as Elizabeth recounted the day's discoveries. Outside the window, her mother's roses—transplanted from St Michael's parish—bloomed in riotous splendour, their fragrance drifting through the open window.

The Bible rested beside her, its margins filled with her father's thoughts, its pages marked with pressed bluebells and memories. From those words, a legacy had been reclaimed. From those pages, a future had been built.

Annabelle Sinclair Woolworth—once orphaned, once fugitive, now beloved wife, mother, and teacher—looked upon her family and knew with certainty that God's providence worked through trials to bring unexpected blessings. The vicar's daughter had come home at last.

THE FIRST CHAPTER OF 'THE BOOKBINDER'S ORPHAN DAUGHTER'

WINTER, 1843

Dust motes danced in the golden shafts of morning light that spilled through the workshop windows. Eleven-year-old Meredith traced her fingers along the spines of newly bound volumes. The wooden shelves creaked beneath the weight of countless stories, their leather bindings gleaming in various shades of burgundy, forest green, and deep blue.

Thomas Aldrich's tools hung in precise rows against the far wall – brass finishing wheels catching glints of sunlight, awls and needles arranged by size, each implement waiting for the next day's work. The polished workbench dominated the centre of the room, its surface marked by years of careful craftsmanship and bearing the subtle indentations of countless hours spent binding precious volumes.

Between the shelves, narrow aisles created a maze of literary treasures. Some books stood proud and tall, while others huddled together, their spines weathered by time and handling. The morning sun painted patterns across the wooden floorboards, highlighting the worn paths where her father paced as he worked.

Meredith closed her eyes and drew in a deep breath. The familiar scent of leather and glue filled her lungs – a complex aroma that spoke of dedication and artistry. Beneath it lay subtler notes: the mustiness of old paper, the sharp tang of brass polish, the earthiness of wood. These smells had become the very essence of home, weaving themselves into her earliest memories.

Outside, London stirred to life. Cart wheels clattered against cobblestones, and voices from Cedar's Printing House next door filtered through the walls. The smell of fresh bread wafted in from Mrs Cooper's Bakery, mingling with the workshop's own distinct perfume. Yet within these walls, time seemed to slow, creating a peaceful haven from the city's chaos.

Meredith gripped the awl with practiced care, her small fingers finding their familiar position on the worn wooden handle. The leather-bound volume before her waited, its signatures arranged in perfect alignment. She drew in a measured breath, steadying her hand.

Her father worked at the opposite end of the bench, his

movements fluid and precise as he stretched deep burgundy Moroccan leather across the boards of a first edition. His weathered hands moved with certainty born from decades of experience, each gesture purposeful and measured.

The awl pierced the thick paper with a satisfying whisper. Meredith guided it through the fold, creating perfect holes at exact intervals. Her father had taught her to feel the rhythm of the work – too close together and the binding would weaken, too far apart and the pages would gap. The stack of signatures beside her grew smaller as she progressed, each one receiving the same careful attention.

She paused between sections, stealing glances at her father's technique. Thomas's fingers danced across the leather, smoothing away air bubbles and ensuring perfect contact with the board beneath. A thin sheen of paste glistened on the material's underside, catching the morning light. His movements held a grace that Meredith hoped to one day achieve – the kind that made difficult work appear effortless.

Her dark hair fell forward, and she tucked it behind her ear with her free hand, leaving a small smudge of glue on her cheek. The awl moved steadily through the next signature, creating another row of precise holes ready for binding.

She looked up again, studying how her father's hands applied just the right pressure to work the leather into the spine's curves. His fingers knew exactly where to press, how to coax the material into embracing the book's form. Meredith's heart swelled with pride as she watched him work, determined to absorb every detail of his mastery.

In the corner, her mother's voice rose and fell like gentle waves. Elizabeth sat in her cherished armchair, the one with roses and vines that had faded into soft whispers of their original vibrancy. Sunlight caught the silver threads in her light brown hair, creating a halo effect that made Meredith's heart squeeze with love.

The leather-bound volume rested in Elizabeth's lap, its pages spread wide beneath her delicate fingers. Her blue eyes danced across the text, bringing Shakespeare's words to life with each carefully crafted phrase. Her alto voice filled every corner of the workshop, wrapping around the tools and books like a warm embrace.

"'What's in a name? That which we call a rose by any other name would smell as sweet.'" Elizabeth's voice carried Romeo's longing, each word precise and measured. She paused, letting the poetry settle in the air between the leather and glue.

Elizabeth shifted in her chair, the worn fabric creaking softly beneath her. The morning light caught the silver locket at her throat, the one containing the miniature picture from her wedding day. Her fingers traced the page's edge with reverence before continuing, her voice rising and falling with the rhythm of the verse.

Meredith's fingers paused on the awl as her mother painted pictures in the morning air. Elizabeth's words transformed the workshop into a Verona street, where star-crossed lovers exchanged promises beneath a moonlit balcony. Her familiar surroundings melded with imagined Italian gardens, creating a world that existed between the reality of their modest workshop and the boundless realm of Shakespeare's creation.

Her mother's silver locket caught the light as she leaned forward, each word precise and measured. The way Elizabeth's fingers traced the pages, treating each leaf with the same care Thomas showed his finest leather bindings, made Meredith's chest tighten with love.

"'Deny thy father and refuse thy name,'" Elizabeth's voice

swelled with emotion, her blue eyes dancing across the text. "'Or, if thou wilt not, be but sworn my love, and I'll no longer be a Capulet.'"

Thomas looked up from his work, burgundy leather forgotten beneath his skilled hands. His eyes met Elizabeth's across the workshop, and something passed between them – a current of understanding that made the air itself seem to shimmer. The corner of his mouth lifted in a tender smile, and Elizabeth's voice grew softer, more intimate, as if the words were meant for him alone.

Meredith watched their exchange, her own heart full. The way her mother brought stories to life, the careful attention her father paid to each binding – these were the threads that wove their family together. She imagined herself someday, reading to children of her own, passing on not just the words but the magic that lived within them.

Elizabeth's voice carried on, steady and clear as a bell, each syllable perfectly formed. Meredith's hands resumed their work, but her mind danced with the poetry, storing away her mother's cadence and inflection like precious treasures.

The awl slipped. Sharp pain shot through Meredith's finger, and a bright bead of blood welled up against her skin. She bit her lip, trapping the gasp in her throat. The perfect line of holes in the signature blurred as tears pricked her eyes.

Thomas's workbench creaked as he set down his tools. His footsteps crossed the workshop floor, and his warm hand settled on her shoulder. "Let me see."

Meredith held out her trembling finger. The drop of blood had grown larger, threatening to fall onto the pristine paper below. Her father's weathered hands cupped her smaller one, turning it in the morning light.

"The awl found you, did it?" Thomas reached for the small

medical kit they kept near the washing basin. "Every bookbinder pays for their craft in blood at some point."

Elizabeth set aside Romeo and Juliet, the poetry forgotten as she rose from her chair. Her skirts rustled as she crossed to Meredith's side. "Your father speaks true. I've bandaged his fingers more times than I can count."

Thomas cleaned the small wound with practiced movements. "The first time I used an awl, I managed to stick myself three times in one afternoon." He wrapped a strip of clean linen around her finger with gentle precision. "Each scar is a lesson learned."

Elizabeth's cool hand brushed Meredith's cheek. "There now. No lasting harm done."

The bandage was snug but not too tight, much like the bindings her father created. Meredith flexed her finger, testing the wrap. The sting had already begun to fade, replaced by a dull throb that matched her heartbeat.

"Thank you," she whispered, looking up at her parents' concerned faces. Their love wrapped around her like the finest Morocco leather, protective and precious.

SHADOWS CREPT across the workshop floor as afternoon light filtered through the windows. Meredith set down her tools and stretched her tired fingers, the small bandage catching on the edge of her sleeve. Around her, leather-bound volumes stood like silent sentinels on the shelves her father had built by hand. Each book held not just its printed story, but the tale of its creation – the careful selection of materials, the precise stitching, the loving attention to every detail.

Her fingertips traced the gold lettering on a nearby spine. The workshop felt alive with possibility, even in the growing dimness. One day, she'd have her own space like this, she decided. A place where she could experiment with new binding techniques, perhaps even create entirely new styles of covers that no one had attempted before.

The clatter of hooves against cobblestones drifted through the open window, accompanied by a chorus of street vendors hawking their wares. Children's laughter rang out — probably the Baker twins chasing each other again, she thought. But inside the workshop, time moved differently.

Meredith breathed deeply, taking in the familiar smells that meant home. This was their sanctuary – every tool hanging in its proper place, every shelf loaded with stories waiting to be bound or mended. Even the worn floorboards beneath her feet felt sacred, marked by years of careful footsteps and dropped threads.

She ran her hand along the smooth surface of her father's workbench, feeling the slight indentations that told the story of countless books brought to life under his skilled hands. The workshop was more than just a place of business – it was the heart of their family, beating steady and strong against the rhythm of London's streets.

Thomas pressed the final gilt letters into the leather spine. The first edition gleamed in the late afternoon light, its burgundy surface catching golden highlights from the workshop windows. Meredith leaned forward, drinking in every detail of the finished work – the perfectly squared corners, the delicate headbands, the precise alignment of the text block.

"Come here, little one." Thomas beckoned her closer, his weathered hands still bearing traces of gold leaf. "See how the spine flexes? That's the mark of proper binding. Each signature we sewed, every station we marked – they all serve a purpose."

Elizabeth set aside her worn copy of Romeo and Juliet, her

eyes bright with maternal pride as she watched them. "You've learned so quickly, darling."

"Your mother's right." Thomas ran his finger along the smooth edge of the cover. "Never forget that every task matters, whether it's making those first holes with the awl or finishing the finest leather. Each step builds upon the last, like verses in a poem."

Meredith's heart swelled as she studied their shared handiwork. The book represented more than just bound pages — it was a testament to their family's dedication to craft. She thought of all the readers who would hold this volume, fingers tracing the same gilt letters she'd watched her father press into place. Their workshop might be small, tucked away on Paternoster Row, but their work would travel far beyond these walls.

Her fingertip brushed against the small bandage, a reminder of her earlier mishap. But now, instead of feeling clumsy, she felt marked — initiated into a legacy of craftspeople who had pricked their fingers and stained their hands in service of binding stories together.

"Thank you," she whispered, though the words felt inadequate to express the depth of her gratitude. This was more than just learning a trade – it was finding her place in a tradition that stretched back generations, each book a bridge between past and future.

Click here to read the rest of 'The Bookbinder's Orphan Daughter'

A tale of craft, courage, and the power of unexpected kindness.

Young Meredith Aldrich's world crumbles when consumption claims her beloved mother and skilled bookbinder father in quick succession. Cast onto London's merciless streets, she carries nothing but her father's prized bookbinding tools and the memory of their craft. When a desperate attempt to find shelter leads her to break into a prestigious house, her life takes an unexpected turn.

Instead of punishment, she finds sanctuary as a maid in the household. But not everyone welcomes this unusual arrangement. As Meredith navigates her new life, she finds herself drawn into a world of books, learning, and unexpected friendships - including with Philip Ashworth, Lord Thornfield's handsome nephew.

When her past on the streets threatens to destroy everything she's built, Meredith must decide whether to retreat into safety or stand firm in defence of her place in this new world.

Can a girl born into trade dare to dream of a future among the nobility? And will her love of craft be enough to bridge the chasm between their two worlds?

Follow Meredith's journey from the humble bookbinding workshop of Paternoster Row to the grand halls of the Thornfield estate in this unforgettable story of a young woman who dares to bind together the torn pages of her own destiny!

'The Bookbinder's Orphan Daughter'

OUR GIFT TO YOU
AS A WAY TO SAY THANK YOU WE WOULD LOVE TO SEND YOU THIS BEAUTIFUL STORY FREE OF CHARGE.

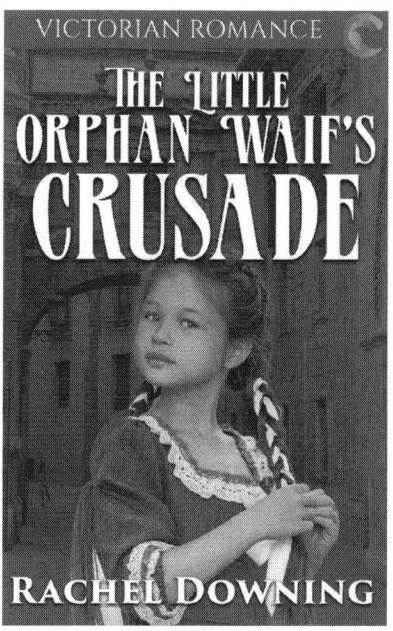

Click here for your FREE COPY of

'The Little Orphan Waif's Crusade'

CornerstoneTales.com/sign-up

In the wake of her father's passing, seven-year-old Matilda is determined to heal her sister Effie's shattered spirit.

Desperate to restore joy to Effie's life, Matilda embarks on a daring quest, aided by the gentle-hearted postman, Philip. Together, they weave a plan to ignite the flame of love in Effie's heart once more.

At Cornerstone Tales we publish books you can trust. Great tales without sex or swearing, but with all of the mystery and romance you expect from a great story.

Be the first to know when we release new books, take part in our fun competitions, and get surprise free books in your inbox by signing up to our free VIP Reader list.

As a thank you you'll receive a copy of 'The Little Orphan Waif's Crusade' by *Rachel Downing* straight away, alongside other gifts.

Click here to sign up for our mailing list, and receive your FREE stories.

CornerstoneTales.com/sign-up

LOVE VICTORIAN ROMANCE?

More Dorothy Welling's Victorian Romance

The Moral Maid's Unjust Trial

Matilda must fend for herself when her father is wrongfully accused for a crime he didn't commit.

Get 'The Moral Maid's Unjust Trial' Here!

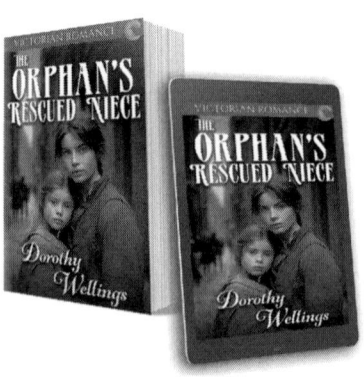

The Orphan's Rescued Niece

As Beatrice grows from a wide-eyed child into a resilient young woman, she finds herself caught between her love for her troubled brother and her desire for a life free from poverty and fear.

Get 'The Orphan's Rescued Niece' Here!

The Bookbinder's Orphan Daughter

Meredith world crumbles when consumption claims her beloved mother and skilled bookbinder father. When a desperate attempt to find shelter leads her to break into a prestigious house, her life takes an unexpected turn.

Get 'The Bookbinder's Orphan Daughter' Here!

Books by our other Victorian Romance Writer *RACHEL DOWNING*

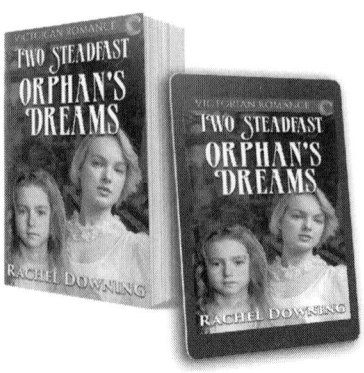

Two Steadfast Orphan's Dreams

Follow the stories of Isabella and Ada as they overcome all odds and find love.

Get 'Two Steadfast Orphan's Dreams' Here!

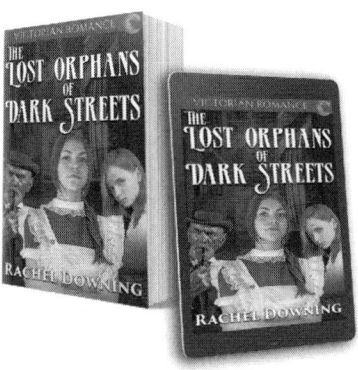

The Lost Orphans of Dark Streets

Follow the stories of Elizabeth and Molly as they negotiate the dangerous slums and find their place in the world.

Get 'The Lost Orphans of Dark Streets' Here!

The Orphan Prodigy's Stolen Tale

When ten-year-old Isabella Farmerson's world shatters with the tragic loss of her parents, she's thrust into a life of hardship and uncertainty.

Get 'The Orphan Prodigy's Stolen Tale' Here!

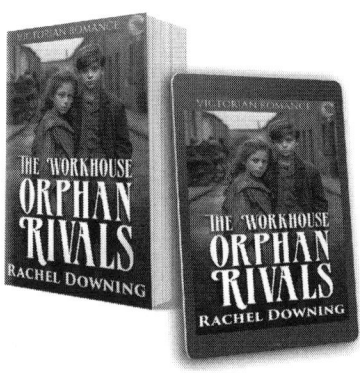

The Workhouse Orphan Rivals

Childhood sweethearts torn apart. A promise broken. A love that refuses to die.

Get 'The Workhouse Orphan Rivals' Here!

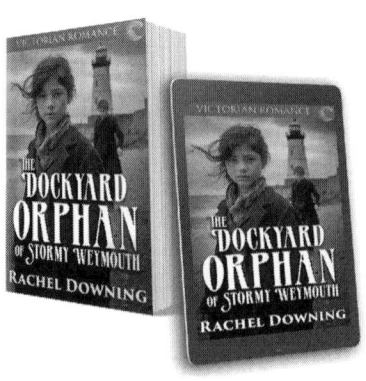

The Dockyard Orphan of Stormy Weymouth

Sarah Campbell's world crumbles when a tragic accident claims her parents' lives. She finds solace in the lighthouse's beam that guides ships to safety. But it's a young fisherman wrestling with his own loss, who truly captures her heart.

Get 'The Dockyard Orphan of Stormy Weymouth' Here!

The Orphan's Christmas Hymn

Seven-year-old Clara Winters' world shatters when tragedy strikes days before Christmas. Sent to St. Mary's Church Orphanage, she finds her only solace in the hymns that once filled her happy home. When her angelic voice catches the attention of the kind-hearted Reverend Thornton and his musically gifted son Edward, Clara dares to dream of a brighter future.

Get 'The Orphan's Christmas Hymn' Here!

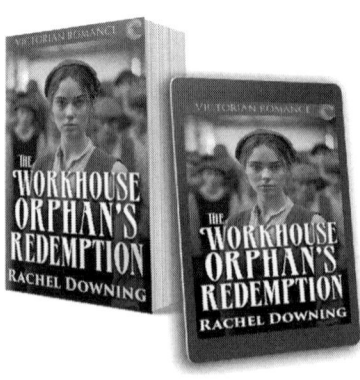

The Workhouse Orphan's Redemption

In the brutal world of Victorian London, Emma Redbrook's life begins in tragedy. Orphaned and trapped in Grimshaw's Workhouse, she endures cruelty that would break most spirits. But Emma's unwavering faith becomes her beacon of hope — and her strength.

Get 'The Workhouse Orphan's Redemption' Here!

The Forsaken Lacemaker of Hampstead

Mabel Fairchild's life is shattered by false accusations and devastating loss. With two younger siblings dependent on her care, she makes an impossible promise: to keep her family together despite the world's cruel intentions.

Get 'The Forsaken Lacemaker of Hampstead' Here!

If you enjoyed this story, sign up to our mailing list to be the first to hear about our new releases and any sales and deals we have.

We also want to offer you a Victorian Romance novella - 'The Little Orphan Waif's Crusade' - absolutely free!

Click here to sign up for our mailing list, and receive your FREE stories.

CornerstoneTales.com/sign-up

Printed in Great Britain
by Amazon